HUGH FLEETWOOD

THE ORDER OF DEATH

SIMON AND SCHUSTER
NEW YORK

Designed by Elizabeth Woll
Manufactured in the United States of America

1   2   3   4   5   6   7   8   9   10

Library of Congress Cataloging in Publication Data

Fleetwood, Hugh.
    The order of death.

    I. Title.
PZ4.F5870r3 [PR6056.L38] 823'.9'14 76-25899
ISBN 0-671-22357-7

For WENDY JACKSON

CHAPTER 1

He glanced up and down the street, slipped sideways up to the newsstand, and looked for the paper that he would pick up and pay for without saying a word; the paper that he picked up and paid for every day, without saying a word. But he couldn't see it. The *Post*, yes, and the *Daily News*. And around the sides of the kiosk, *The Village Voice*, and *Screw*, and *Scum*. But not . . .

He felt the beginning of sweat on his neck under his cashmere scarf. It always made him panic slightly when he had to ask. He wondered if he should go to another newsstand. But then he told himself not to be ridiculous. Today was the day for *this* newsstand, and he couldn't, he mustn't, break the rules. As soon as one started breaking even the smallest rule, chaos broke out. That was a fact. He looked around again—there was only a soft-looking youth by his side, with lank fair hair, staring dopily at the magazines. He leaned toward the old man inside the stand, who was watching him coolly—no doubt expecting him to be searching for some undisplayed dirty book, and murmured in his neat, prim voice, "The *Times*."

"Pardon me?"

Now he felt real sweat under his scarf, and in the palms of his hands too. He would have to ask again! But at least, when he looked around once more, he saw that the youth had gone, and he was alone. He said quickly and more loudly, *"The New York Times."*

"It's finished," the old man rasped.

He swallowed hard and took a step backward. He was so angry he would have liked to hit the old man. But he didn't, of course; he merely let himself be caught up in the tide of people sweeping along the street, and drifted along with it, trembling. Then he slipped his change back into the pocket of his coat and took a tiny diary and a tinier pencil from his briefcase. That newsstand would have to be struck off his list, he told himself. It was absurd—to be out of the *Times* by eleven in the morning! What was more, he couldn't stand insolence. Not in anyone. And especially not in old men.

He opened the diary as he walked, turned to February 9, and crossed out the neat entry "N.Y. Public Library, 42nd St." Then he turned to March 9 and crossed out the same entry. Later, he would select another newsstand to visit on the ninth day of each month, and write that one in.

Meanwhile, he still had to find a *Times* somewhere today. Grand Central Station was the best bet, he guessed, especially as he was drifting in that direction. There were two or three book stalls there, and one of them must have the *Times*. And with so many people about . . .

He glanced over his shoulder and crossed the street.

As soon as he had bought it, he went into a telephone booth and skimmed the paper quickly until he saw a headline that read "No New Developments in Police Murders"; then he folded it up, put it in his briefcase, and left the phone booth to start the journey home.

In theory, this journey from Grand Central Station involved only one change on the subway. But today, perhaps because the incident at the regular newsstand had upset him, or perhaps because he sensed more menace than usual in the crowds around him and felt he had to be particularly careful, he changed twice—and once even had to get off one train and wait on the same platform until the next came in. There hadn't been enough people on the first train, and those that were there had seemed to look at him more than was necessary or normal; they had been too aware of him. . . .

And when he arrived at the West 72nd Street station, he waited until all the other passengers who had gotten off had left the platform before leaving it himself; before climbing the stairs to brave the cold, and the wind, and the brief apprehensive walk along Central Park West.

He only relaxed and became himself when he had passed through his street door, returned the "Good morning" of the doorman, taken the elevator up to the fifth floor, opened his door, and locked it again behind him. Only then could he tell himself that his precautions against being seen and followed were absurd, and that his furtive daily ritual of buying *The New York Times* verged on madness. After all, he thought as he walked, large and confident now, through the huge, warm, empty rooms of his apartment, he was hardly alone in his choice of newspaper, and he was sure nobody *was* following him. What was more, he certainly wasn't a nervous man at any other time of the day or night. He had faced gunmen and knife-wielding addicts without a moment's fear, and generally inspired awe in most people just by looking at them. And so—he made what he called a smile and went into his bathroom and began to strip off his cheap suit. He couldn't explain it. Yet the strange thing, he thought, was that he actually enjoyed that half-hour or hour of tension, that feeling of being hunted and helpless and spied upon, almost as much as he enjoyed anything in his life. It was like being given a blood transfusion. He enjoyed the sweat under his scarf—that scarf that was the only piece of expensive clothing he allowed himself to wear outside of this apartment—and he enjoyed the smell that he gave off, though he was sure that only he could smell it.

In fact, the only thing he did enjoy more than the ritual of getting to his apartment was the apartment itself, and his being there.

And now he *was* there, and he was taking a shower, and when he had finished his shower he would take a white silk shirt that he had had made for him and put it on, and he would put on the gray silk suit that he had had made for him, and the black silk socks, and the crocodile-skin shoes, and one of his ten silk ties, and he would look at himself in the mirror: look at his strong, enormous body in its fine clothes; at his square reddish face with its short reddish hair and its bright red eyebrows; and at his big red hands. And then he would close his eyes and stand there and just for a minute feel quite sick with the joy of being alive.

Then he would go into the room overlooking the park that would have been, that should have been, and in a way was, the living room, and take a bottle of fine whiskey from the cabinet and pour himself a drink. Then he would sit down in one of the two brown leather armchairs that were—not counting the kitchen—the only other pieces of furniture in the whole apartment, and would sip his whiskey and look at the fresh white walls and the deep greenish-brown carpet, and read *The New York Times*. He would sit there for an hour or two, and then he would get up and take off his fine clothes and fold them up neatly and put them away. Then he would put on his old cheap clothes again, do some cleaning, and, finally, leave—to go, depending on whether he had come to the apartment before going on duty or after coming off, either to work or to the small shabby apartment on the first floor of a shabby brownstone in Brooklyn where he actually lived.

Every day of the year, barring accidents, he did precisely the same thing, except for the weeks of his vacation, and then he would spend all day at the apartment, and would eat there, and would return to Brooklyn only to sleep.

Today, however, after he had showered and dressed, the perfection of pleasure that his time in the apartment gave him was marred slightly: when he went into the kitchen to get a glass for his whiskey, he saw crumbs on the sideboard, and spilled milk on the stove. For a second he felt as angry as he had when the vendor had told him that the *Times* was finished. But then he forced himself to think— since nothing as ugly as anger must be allowed to intrude into this paradise of his—that a few crumbs and a bit of milk were nothing to worry about. So he took off his jacket, put it on a hanger that was behind the kitchen door, undid his gold cuff links, rolled up the sleeves of his silk shirt, and, taking a cloth from under the sink, carefully swept up the crumbs and cleaned the stove. When everything was spotless, he took a sharpened pencil and a piece of paper from a drawer and wrote in a small neat hand:

Bob,
    I guess you were hungry and had a snack and some coffee or something. But you left crumbs on the sideboard and spilled milk on the stove. I guess you were in a hurry, or you would have cleaned up after you. But please do not leave a mess. You know I don't like a mess.

Fred

He checked the note, approved it—its tone was suitably ingenuous—and left it in the center of the sideboard, where the crumbs had been. Then he took a pencil sharpener from the drawer, sharpened his pencil over the sink, replaced both sharpener and pencil in the drawer, turned on the waste-disposal unit and cleaned out the sink, dried his hands, rolled down his sleeves and fixed his cuff links, put on his jacket again, and took the glass that he had come into the kitchen to fetch.

He hoped he wouldn't have any more trouble with Bob—for a while, at least. And he probably wouldn't, he thought. In part because Bob, in spite of his condescending attitude toward him, was scared of him, and in part because Bob only rarely came to the apartment now. In fact, ever since he had married, a year and a half ago, he had been coming less and less—and Fred foresaw a time when he wouldn't come at all any more. Which would be nice, he reflected. Then this place would be all his, and there would be no danger of finding crumbs in the kitchen—or, as he had done once, hair and scum in one of the bathtubs. God, he remembered that! It was just over a year ago. He had gone into Bob's bathroom for some reason, and had never seen anything so filthy, so sacrilegious, in his life. Not only had there been scum and hair in the bathtub, but also toothpaste in the washbasin, shit in the toilet bowl, and a damp towel lying on the floor. Bob had protested that it was his bathroom, but that was no excuse. He had exploded and told Bob that if anything like that ever happened again their partnership would be over; he would buy out Bob's share of the apartment, or even tell Lenore about their mutual investment.

And Bob would have done anything rather than let that happen. . . .

It was because he hated a mess, he told himself as he settled into his armchair with his whiskey and started to open the paper, that he hated *The New York Times*, and was so ashamed of buying it that he changed newsstands every day in case anyone should get to know him, and pigeonhole him as a man who read the *Times*. It was a paper that championed mess and disorder. In fact, he had often thought that the troubles there had been and were in the city of New York—with blacks, and hoodlums, and addicts—were all caused by the sort of people who read the *Times;* people who had been so conditioned into feeling guilty that they had invented punishment for themselves—punishment that took the form of gangsters and muggers and delinquents. The only trouble was that everyone else had to share in their punishment, too. Which wasn't fair.

It was because the *Times* was the enemy newspaper that he felt he should read it—as a form of defense, just to know what the enemy was up to. And especially now.

He opened it at the page he had found in the telephone booth, and started to read.

Police Commissioner Barnes said at a press conference today that the police have discovered no new evidence to help them with their investigation into the murder last Tuesday of Detective Jim Parro. Commissioner Barnes did say, however, that there is no doubt that Officer Parro was the latest victim of the assassin who has now been responsible for the deaths of five city police officers over the last eighteen months, all of whom were attached to the Narcotics Bureau. Detective Parro was found in the hallway of a building on East 4th Street. His throat had apparently been cut—as the other four victims' throats were cut—with a bread knife.

Poor Jim, Fred thought. He stopped reading for a moment and gazed out the window, where one or two flakes of snow were now aimlessly drifting up and down in the February wind. He wondered if it had hurt. He ran a finger over his own throat, and imagined a bread knife sawing into that hard, thick skin, and shivered.

But then he thought of Jim again, as he had seen him,

lying in that dark brown hallway, with his throat grinning and his cheap clothes all stained and dirty with blood, and once more he shivered. At least if he died a violent death he hoped it would be here, in his secret kingdom, and with his fine clothes on. Then, somehow, it wouldn't be so bad. But he didn't think he would die a violent death. He wasn't, surely, the type. No—he would go on working for another ten years or so, and then, with enough coming in from his carefully invested money, he would retire here and spend his days tending and nursing his apartment, slowly furnishing it, keeping it clean, looking after it as if it were his child. He would go for a walk every day—across the park and back maybe; from eleven to twelve—and then would come back, make himself some lunch, and spend the afternoons reading his encyclopedias; article after article, volume after volume, slowly, carefully, taking all that knowledge in, stacking it tidily on the shelves of his mind. And in the evenings he would have his supper and watch the television and read *The Wall Street Journal* and make sure his stocks were doing all they should be doing. And sometimes, just occasionally, he would go out at night and wander around—go down to the Village maybe, or to Times Square—and look at all the great sprawling filthy chaos of people, cars, and refuse; look at them just to reassure himself, just to value all the more his isolation, his peace, his order. He would have no friends; he never had had any, unless Bob had once been a friend; but he didn't think so; his relationship with Bob was just a mistake he bitterly regretted. And he would speak to no one except the storekeepers and a few other people like that. He sighed. How he longed for that time! But then he reminded himself that the minutes were passing and he still hadn't finished looking at the *Times;* so he picked it up again and, once more, started reading.

When he had finished the piece about Jim's murder, he

went to the front page and worked his way systematically through the paper, reading almost every article, skipping hardly a word, only saving till last an editorial headed "The Dead Policemen."

The brutal murder of Detective Parro and his four colleagues raises three equally terrifying suspicions. One, that there is a maniac on the loose who enjoys murdering policemen attached to the Narcotics Bureau. Two, that organized crime has changed its rules and has taken to the attack, rather than, as has always been the case with regard to the police, maintaining a generally very effective defense. And three, that the five murdered officers were killed by a member or members of their own force who perhaps feared that their investigations into the narcotics scene would uncover more than just a ring of dealers and pushers. And it is this last suspicion that is perhaps the most disquieting. That police corruption exists, always has existed, and probably always will exist is an unfortunate state of affairs that we have had to come, grimly, to accept. That corruption no longer involves merely the acceptance of bribes but might also involve the death of any man who is foolhardy enough to refuse to be corrupted is a new and horrific development, a presage of a state of total anarchy, when no officer will dare to refuse the lucrative offers made to him, for fear that to do so will be, quite literally, to cut his own throat.

Fred sipped his whiskey and threw the paper down on the floor. He couldn't be bothered to go on reading. What was the point of wading through all that nonsense when the editor obviously had no idea what he was talking about? Anarchy! Corruption! They were all such grand, pompous words. How could anyone talk about corruption when drugs were involved? If there was anything on earth guaranteed to keep order, it was drugs and drug addiction, and if there was anything noble in the world, it was the propagation, by whatever means, of drugs. It was the ban-

15

ning, the illegality of drugs, that caused crime, and it was, ultimately, the banning and illegality of drugs that had caused the death of Jim and the others—who hadn't had the sense to see that by fighting drugs they were fighting the very order they sought to uphold. Drugs should be available to all, should be given away to anyone who wanted them. Then all the trash and rottenness of society would be under control, would behave themselves and do as they were told—do as they were told by the strong, by those who had no need of drugs. Oh, yes—all the great civilizations of the past had been slave societies, and this society, this America, would not only be greater and stronger than any of the civilizations of the past if it realized this: it would also last longer, far longer, if not forever. As it was, it was corrupted and ruled by the weak, who were worming away at the foundations, encouraged in their destructiveness by the pillars of bad conscience and the spokesmen of guilt, such as the writers and readers of papers like *The New York Times*. The weak were the true corruptors! The beauty of a society in which drugs were freely available would be that its slaves would be voluntary slaves, not slaves who had been captured and branded and forced into slavery. And they would be slaves who could at any moment, if they were strong enough, stop being slaves; could, with an effort of will, join the ranks of the strong. The only people on whom drugs perhaps should be forced would be those few found guilty of crimes committed when they were not on drugs. But these would be so few they would be negligible. And as soon as they were addicted they could be released from prison—six months would be the longest sentence necessary for anyone—and could become members of the great, law-abiding army of the weak, whose terrible punishment if *they* ever broke the law would be the immediate withdrawal of their precious, life-giving powder. But drugged criminals would be even fewer than the undrugged ones; after all, they would be given food, clothing, and shelter—and what else would they need, apart from their daily or hourly shot? Of course it would be necessary to find the best drug for each person, just in case certain drugs incited certain subjects to violence, but that would be easy enough.

He was shaking, and he stood up and went over to the window and calmed himself by looking down over the granite hillocks of the park, at the people hurrying along the sidewalk, and at the snow that was starting to fall more heavily now and settle. He breathed in deeply and told himself that he really shouldn't have these fantasies; they agitated him and were bad for him, because he knew they were just fantasies, and crazy fantasies too. And yet there was some sort of truth in them, he was convinced, even if it was only a sort of poetic truth; and what was more, he did, quite rationally, approve of drug-taking, because it *did* make the weak . . . no! He mustn't start again. He mustn't think about such things. That too—the indulging of idle fantasies—was weakness. Let them call him a corrupt cop if they wanted to, let them say that this apartment and his slowly growing number of stocks were the fruits of his corruption. Let them call him what they wanted, and let them forget that if it weren't for him, and people like him, there would be still more violence and crime than there was. Let them call him what they wanted; they were the weak and guilty. He wouldn't, he couldn't, be bothered with them.

He picked up the paper, folded it again, and put it in his briefcase; later he would throw it away. Then he glanced at his watch, saw that it was almost time to go, and went to change.

He was just putting on his old cheap trousers when something odd happened. Something odd and very disturbing. First of all, his house phone rang—something that happened about once a year normally, and then generally only because Bob was passing by for some reason, couldn't be bothered to come up, and was just calling up from the lobby to say hi, or to tell him something. And then, secondly, when he softly, suspiciously answered, the doorman told him there was "a Mr. Smith" to see him.

"For *me?*" Fred asked, and again, as earlier at the newsstand, he felt sweat break out on the back of his neck and in the palms of his hands.

"Yes, sir," the doorman said.

"Are you sure?" He was not only sweating but feeling sick now.

He heard the doorman smile. "Yes, sir." Then, more faintly, he heard him inquire, "It was Mr. Fred O'Connor you said?"

He didn't hear anyone say anything. Then the doorman spoke to him again.

"Yes, sir. It's you."

"Who did you say it was?"

"Mr. Smith."

He heard a murmur.

"Mr. Leo Smith."

"I'm sorry. There must be some mistake. I don't know any Smith. And I'm busy. Could you ask Mr. Smith to write me if he wants to see me?"

"Yes, sir," the doorman said for the last time.

Fred backed away from the phone, staring at it as if it were a dangerous animal. And then he looked wildly around at his corridor, at his walls, at his open doors leading into empty rooms, and he thought he would pass out. The walls seemed to waver and become insubstantial, the empty rooms to dissolve. His secret palace, his secret life, his unassailable fortress—unassailable because it was *secret*—was being threatened. It was impossible. Someone looking for him. For *him?* And a Mr. Smith—he didn't know any Mr. Smith! How *could* it have happened? He backed, lurching now, big and red and frightened, all the way back to the room overlooking the park, and sat down in one of the armchairs. All his precautions had been in vain. Someone had followed him. Someone knew where he lived. He started to shake his head back and forth, as if to fling what he had just discovered out of it. Then he gripped the sides of the armchair and told himself to keep still. He bit his lower lip, bit it savagely, and forced himself to keep still. Then he thought—Bob. Yes. That was it. Someone must have followed Bob one day, because Bob never took any precautions at all when he came here—he always said he couldn't see why he should. He just took the subway or the bus, and walked casually up to the door. Bob never took the secret path, as it were, to the secret palace; and now he had led the enemy there. And with his carelessness he had threatened four years—no, fifteen years —of planning, and saving, and safety. Goddamn him. *Goddamn* him. Fred would kill him when he saw him. He would!

But if Mr. Smith, whoever he was, had followed Bob, *why hadn't he asked for Bob?* He looked out the window and felt a depression falling on him as heavily and deeply as the snow outside. No. It wasn't Bob's fault. It was *his* fault. But what had he done wrong? What more precautions could he have taken? He shook his head again, though slowly now, knowing that he could shake nothing out of it.

Then he stood up and went to finish dressing.

Maybe, he thought, Mr. Smith was someone entirely innocuous. A salesman. Someone from an insurance company. No. He would have asked for Mr. Frank O'Connor— Frank, which was his real name, not Fred, which he was always called. Besides, what insurance agent or salesman was ever called Smith? No. Mr. Smith was the enemy. The

Enemy. He was absolutely certain. Mr. Smith was weakness. He was disorder. He was crumbs in the kitchen, *The New York Times*, the representative, not of any company or corporation, but of the guilty. He was the Bad Conscience. He was the worm eating at the base of this great, strong, safe dream that was America. He was . . . Fred paused as he knotted his cheap black tie. He was, possibly, waiting down in the lobby. Or if not in the lobby, then across the street. Or in some doorway farther down the block.

He breathed in deeply. Well, if he was, he would face him. He would go out onto the field of battle and meet him, and beat him, whoever he was. He wasn't afraid of Mr. Smith or anyone else. He couldn't be. Because if he were afraid now, he might lose everything. And he wasn't going to. Not now. Not for any Mr. Smith on earth.

He pulled his jacket on, folded up his clothes (his real clothes), carefully put them away, wrapped his scarf around his neck, looked at himself in the mirror in the bathroom to reassure himself that he was still a giant—a great man, six feet six inches tall, thick and strong, red as a warrior and, at thirty-eight, at the peak of his power and his manhood—and then walked grimly to his front door, opened it, and locked it behind him, remembering just at the very last minute to whisper a silent farewell to his apartment.

In the lobby, he asked the small, plump, pale young doorman if Mr. Smith had left any message. He tried to make the question sound entirely casual.

"No, sir. He said it wasn't important, and he would come by again some other time when you weren't busy."

"What was he like?"

"I couldn't really tell you. He was young, I guess. But he

had one of those wool caps pulled down over his ears, and a scarf all up around his face, and dark glasses."

Fred nodded and, with a great effort, managed a visible smile. To give what would be recognized by the outside world as a smile always cost him a great effort. And then, with an even greater effort, he managed to say slowly, "I guess he was someone from my ex-wife. She occasionally sends spies to check up on me."

He glanced at the doorman to see what effect this lie would have. He hoped it would be greeted with proper indifference. Instead it prompted an understanding nod, which made him feel angry first with the doorman—how did he dare to presume to understand him?—and secondly with himself for having lowered himself, for having lied. Why had he bothered to explain? Why hadn't he just asked what he wanted to ask and then walked out with a polite nod, as he normally did? But then, to make matters worse, he added, quite involuntarily and without being able to check himself, "If he comes again, just tell him I'm not in, will you?"

"Yes, sir," the doorman said, and now, slyly and with an air of complicity, the doorman smiled at him.

He walked out into the street, without even acknowledging the doorman's "Have a good day, sir."

It was only much later, when sitting at his desk in the headquarters of the Narcotics Bureau, playing the part of Lieutenant O'Connor—a large, precise officer with a shy, stern, if slightly old-maidish manner and a hatred of confusion; a soft-spoken man who had worked his way through college and had an ex-wife living in Denver; a man who was respected for his record and his dedication, in spite of a suspicion that his occasional fraternizing with the upper crust of the criminal classes went above and beyond the call of duty (though there was no evidence that he did it for financial gain; no one had ever seen him accept a bribe, and, after all, his suits really were pretty cheap, he didn't own a car, he never went away on vacation, and the few men who had seen the apartment where he lived in Brooklyn had been surprised by its austereness and, for such a fastidious man, its shabbiness); and a man who was not known to have any interests, friends, or hobbies outside his work—that he realized he had forgotten to wash his whiskey glass before he left the apartment.

CHAPTER 2

He decided to return there after he went off duty. And if this morning he had taken precautions, now he was doubly, triply cautious. He took a taxi; he changed to the subway; he took another taxi. He lurked in doorways to see if there was anyone following; he stood in phone booths, his feet cold with the snow, and pretended to call someone.

It was just before midnight when he arrived at his building; there was a doorman he had seen only once or twice before on duty, and he didn't think there was any point in asking him if Mr. Smith had called for him again. But when he took the elevator up and unlocked his door, there was a light on in the apartment.

He allowed himself just a second of doubt, of panic; then he settled down, more comfortably, into anger.

It was Bob. It had to be Bob. He always hated Bob's being here. It was bad enough knowing that he came, but to actually meet him here . . . He hated to be reminded that his kingdom wasn't quite exclusive. And what did it mean—Bob's coming twice in two days?

He walked softly down the corridor toward the kitchen, where the light was coming from, and wondered if Bob had heard him come in. He hoped not. It would be nice to give him a shock; nice to see, if only for a moment, fear in *his* face, too.

When he got to the door of the kitchen, and stood there, Bob didn't seem to be aware of him. He was calmly, gravely spreading some peanut butter on a slice of bread, gazing at it sadly as he did so, as if it were one of the sick, underprivileged, exploited souls his heart was always bleeding for.

Fred coughed.

Bob looked up, his soft handsome face—his weak, actor's face—collapsing slightly into a smile; his brown mournful eyes flickering with just a shade—not so much that he could be accused of it, but just enough to be offensive—of pity.

"Hi, Fred," he said, as if addressing a patient in a hospital—or in a madhouse.

Fred didn't move and didn't reply, trying to think of something to say that would remove that shadow of pity from Bob's eyes; trying to think of some way of smashing that mask of condescension and exposing the fear that he knew lay behind. He stared at the crumbs lying once again on the sideboard, and thought that they might provide him with an excuse.

"Sorry about the crumbs," Bob said. "I'll clean up when I'm through. I saw your note." He smiled again, as if he felt he had to humor his patient.

And he managed to embarrass Fred, make him regret that he had left the note, or at least the consciously ignorant tone of it.

"How come you're here?"

"Lenore's gone to visit her mother. She's sick," Bob added sadly.

"No one followed you here, did they?"

"No. Of course not," Bob said, taking his patient's fears seriously, and brushing them gravely, understandingly away. "Why?"

24

"I just wondered."

He didn't want to tell Bob about Mr. Smith. Because Mr. Smith concerned *him*, and had asked for *him*, and if he told Bob, Bob would think that *he* hadn't been careful. Mr. Smith was someone he'd handle by himself.

He turned and walked on down the corridor to the living room. The light was on there too, and as Fred gazed toward the armchair where he had sat that morning, he heard Bob call reassuringly from the kitchen, "If you're looking for your glass, I washed it."

He sat down and closed his eyes. Oh, God, how he hated Bob. Hated hated hated him. Maybe Mr. Smith was a joke of Bob's—someone sent to scare him, to disturb him, to spoil his paradise. He clutched the arms of the chair. Oh, how he would love to kill Bob. To get him out of this apartment forever. He hated hated and hated him. And he hated himself for having been weak once in his life, for having once been taken in by Bob. And yet, he told himself wretchedly, if it hadn't been for Bob, he wouldn't be here at all now. . . .

Bob hadn't been the first person to discover secret depths in him, to guess that somewhere buried in that great red Irish hulk there was a small, odd flame burning. In fact, quite a lot of people had realized it. His superiors, for instance—which was why his promotion had been so rapid. Of course his college degree had helped, and his efficiency, and his record, and the exams he had taken. But other people had college degrees and good records and hadn't risen as quickly as he. No, he was sure it was because, unconsciously maybe, they had felt that flame in him and, probably even more unconsciously, had been afraid of it; afraid of what might happen if it wasn't given a little more air, a little more space to breathe in, to burn more brightly and less dangerously. And then his financiers —those old-fashioned gentlemen with European accents and big houses on Long Island, who catered to the weak, who sold stock, as it were, in slavery—they too had guessed, quite early on, the existence of that flame in this unlikely-looking material, and had realized that, if properly fed, it could well power and propel a strange, intense craft that would be useful to them and be their defense. And then again, Lenore, who had come to interview him for a series of snappy, satirical little articles about the police that she was writing for *New York* magazine. Instead of getting some easy copy from her meeting with what she had hoped would be an archetypal, quintessential pig, she had gotten so near that flame that her paper had been charred before she ever set pen to it, and she had very nearly been burned herself. But no one, ever, apart from Bob, had seen that flame in him the very first time they laid eyes on him. Yet Bob˙ had seen it as a hawk sees a fieldmouse; and he had swooped on it. He had gone straight to it and hadn't been afraid for a second. Within an hour of meeting Fred, he had exposed it and made it flare up more brightly than even Fred himself would have thought possible. They had been on the Lower East Side together—two plainclothes cops, one looking like an Irish construction worker, and the other, newly transferred into the Narcotics Bureau, like his kid brother up from the country. They were watching a black pusher who was too big for the Commissioner but not big enough for the gentlemen from Long Island to want to save. In the line of duty, they had entered a grimy bar on Avenue B to have a drink. And there, sitting in a corner of that sordid saloon, with two cans of beer on the rickety wooden table between them, while they kept watch on a house opposite through a diamond-paned window, they had talked.

Or rather, Fred had talked. He had told Bob all about his huge, asthmatic, alcoholic father, who used to beat up his wife, Fred's mother, and died by choking on his own vomit one hot summer evening after he had drunk, one after another, fourteen cans of beer. He had told Bob all about his mother, a tall, thin, proud, well-educated woman, who had almost died giving birth to her only son and had never forgiven him for the pain she had suffered. She had always loved the wheezing wreck of a sea lion she had married, even when he beat her—smashing, over the years, her left arm three times, her right arm once, all her front teeth, her nose and nine of her ribs—loved him even when she was so tired from working, cleaning, cooking and fighting that she couldn't, by the time she went to bed, stop the tears that poured silently out of her eyes, as if some pipe had broken in her head and she no longer had the strength to repair it. She cried especially long and hard when her son, who by the time he was twelve was stronger than his ruined father, attacked him, generally with words, but sometimes physically too. He had told Bob all about their apartment in the Bronx that reeked of drink and vomit and piss the whole time, but always had clean white antimacassars on the three old chairs they owned. In the bathroom there was a statue of the Madonna with eyes that lit up, and there were a lot of books in a big old bookcase which his obsessively clean mother never dusted, so as not to remind herself of what had happened to her education. He had told Bob about his school days, about the fear he had inspired in the other kids, and the even greater fear he had inspired in his teachers when they realized that this unattractive, unsympathetic, sullen lump was no fool—was even, in fact, rather bright, and possibly quite clever. He had told Bob about his loneliness as a child, a feeling he had never recognized as loneliness until he had run across the definition of the word in a dictionary, and how, because he had never had a single friend, he had never really missed having friends. He had told Bob how he had put himself through college, supporting himself by working for one year as a construction hand, and for two as—don't laugh, he got the job through an employment agency after telling the unbelieving man at the desk that he could draw quite well, or at least neatly—an assistant to a mad old arthritic Frenchman who was writing an unpublishable book about butterflies and wanted someone to make drawings of every known species of butterfly, and to lift and carry about the glass display cases in which the butterflies, many of them moth-eaten, were pinned out, and to act as a sort of sorcerer's apprentice. The old Frenchman had been mean, ill-tempered and unpleasant, and in the two years Fred worked for him they hardly exchanged more than fifty words; but whether because he was too frightened of Fred to send him away or simply because he was satisfied with his assistant, the Frenchman had kept him on until he graduated. After he graduated he did his military service, and then decided to join the police.

He had told Bob how he met Helen. She had been a typist at the precinct station, and he had been attracted to her first because of her uncomplaining, or uncomprehending, friendlessness. He guessed they were happy together, even if they both felt that theirs was in a way an arranged marriage, like marriages in the old days, and that he should call her Mrs. O'Connor when he spoke to her, instead of Helen. "Helen," was somehow too informal. But—and he had even told Bob this, which was surprising, because he was really very shy, not to say prudish, about such things —they had a satisfactory sex life together, and she was a good cook and very tidy, so he had no reason to complain.

Finally, over another can of beer, encouraged by Bob's silence, he had told about his vision and his fear: about his dream of a society in which the weak and guilty were allowed, or encouraged, to destroy themselves so that for the rest, for the strong and innocent, there would be peace and freedom; and about his terror—a terror so strong at times that he felt himself being consumed by it—that this dream, this vision, never being allowed to flower, never having any chance of becoming reality (for he realized that by now it was too late for society to go anywhere but downward into chaos and destruction), would either go bad within him and become madness, or worse, would die altogether, crushed by the outside world, killed by a lack of air. And if that happened, he would be left with only the great hulk of his own body, and with other people's ideas and opinions of him. He would become a vast, dumb zombie; he would cease to exist. Because, he whispered urgently, passionately, leaning toward the silent Bob, clutching his empty beer can and forgetting to keep even half an eye on the window, his dream was the only thing that kept him alive, was the only thing that was, really, *him.* His beautiful dream of an ordered, planned world, where everything was written down, prescribed, so that one merely had to follow the steps as in the most rigidly choreographed dance; steps that could always be improved and polished over the years, until the dance was perfect. . . .

Oh, sure (he had said defensively, and not really believing it), he knew it wasn't a very original dream, and it was probably full of holes—but it was his, and he clung to it, and he would fight for it to the death, and he was terrified of losing it. If only, he had said quite loudly in his awkwardness, we had space within ourselves where we could keep our dreams—where they could grow peacefully and be absolutely safe from destruction; where we could go and visit them and look after them; where we could love them. . . . Oh, if only, if only we had space within.

And then at last he had sat back in his seat in that shabby bar on Avenue B, looked up again at the window he was supposed to be watching, and waited for Bob to talk to *him;* to give him some proof that this secret, tender life he had pulled out and shown was not going to be abused; to reassure him that he had not, by revealing himself, put himself in danger of some knife of mockery or contempt.

But Bob had told him only one thing. Sadly, as if it were a tragic condition of life rather than a choice he had made, he had told Fred that he, Bob Garitano, accepted bribes, and was, in short, a corrupt cop.

At which, Fred had laughed.

But Bob hadn't seemed to hear him; at least he hadn't taken any notice of him. He had said—and if this was meant as a proof of his trustworthiness, Fred would have preferred not to hear it—that he had always resisted until two years before, when his father had been found to have cancer and needed an urgent, and expensive, operation. At exactly the same moment, he had had a great deal of money almost flung at him by certain important people who needed some help in relation to a case involving ten- and eleven-year-old prostitutes. Bob had taken the money, and his father had died before he could have his operation. It had been sort of ironic. And ever since, every now and then after that first betrayal, he had accepted bribes—almost as if to punish himself, he had said bitterly to Fred, for having accepted the first one.

And Fred, who at any other time would have laughed at this too, hadn't then, and strangely, in fact, had believed him.

And when Bob had gone on to say that he often wondered what to do with all the money he had gotten (which was just collecting interest in some bank, for he didn't have expensive tastes) and that he had often thought it should be invested some better way (after all, since it existed, there was no point in pretending it didn't, and one might just as well make the best of it), Fred hadn't even laughed at that, at that evidence of just how sorry Bob was, and just how easily people could accommodate their morality where money was involved. He hadn't laughed

30

at it, nor had he even thought that Bob was, according to his standards, one of the weak and guilty; one of the despicable; one of the truly corrupt. No. He had simply sat, looking out the window, and waited.

And when Bob, taking it for granted that he too was corrupt, had asked him what he thought of the idea of their going into partnership together and buying some real estate that would be a good investment, he had nodded and answered, "Great."

It was only after they had bought the apartment on Central Park West and had more or less moved in that Fred realized (a) that he had found the space he needed for his dream to be safe in, and that (b) Bob, apart from being weak and guilty and corrupt, was also, appallingly, *sorry* for him; he had spotted that flame in Fred and had breathed on it and fanned it simply because he had thought it was a desperate, terrible signal for help. And he just loved to help the desperate. . . .

Fred had been so enraged when he realized this—enraged at Bob, but even more so at himself for having been taken in—that he had insisted on the peculiar terms of their use, or nonuse, of the apartment, and laid down so many rules and regulations that the apartment, instead of being an investment or a pleasure for Bob, was simply a drain on his income. The monthly maintenance payments were high. Fred had done all this hoping that Bob would fight; would say he wanted to get out of their agreement and their partnership, and leave the apartment to him alone. But Bob hadn't. Without a murmur of protest, with just the occasional soft smile of one who *really* understands, he had agreed to everything. And he had agreed, Fred was certain, because he felt that this way he was both being properly punished for his crimes and—the ultimate act of charity—providing asylum for a soul in agony. It was as if Fred were both his guilty conscience and his pet lunatic;

his own private, special patient, to whom only he could go, and to whom only he could minister. The more he thought about it, the more Fred became convinced this was why Bob had made the suggestion in the first place. On the other hand, if it *hadn't* been for Bob . . .

He sat for a while longer in the armchair in the living room, and then stood up, went down the corridor, past the kitchen, and, without saying a word to Bob, let himself out and closed the door behind him.

Next morning he returned to the apartment before going on duty. He had been there only fifteen minutes and was just drying himself after his shower when the doorman called up and told him that a Mr. Smith was in the lobby waiting to see him. Fred exploded, shouting over the phone that he had said only yesterday that he was not at home to anyone, that he was not to be disturbed for any reason. The doorman sounded puzzled, and apologized; and as he did so, Fred realized that it was not the same doorman as yesterday. How many of them were there, for God's sake? He apologized himself for his outburst, and asked that all the doormen be given instructions that he was not to be disturbed.

The doorman murmured that Mr. Smith said he had to see him urgently. He insisted.

Quietly now, Fred repeated that he was not at home to anyone—to *anyone*. Was that clear?

"Yes, sir."

Fred intended to go to a window of one of the rooms overlooking the street, to see if he could get a glimpse of this Smith as he left. But before he got to the window, or even into the room, he felt so sick he had to go into the bathroom and vomit.

He was in the bathroom for ten minutes, retching into

the toilet. When he came out he felt too tired, too depressed to go and change, to go and put on his fine suit and pour himself a glass of whiskey. So he sat on the floor of the corridor and rested his head against the wall and didn't move; didn't move until he suddenly realized that there were tears running down his wide, rough red cheek. Then he wearily lifted an arm and wiped his eyes.

He and Bob rarely saw each other when they were on duty, and even more rarely spoke to each other; and when they did, it was strictly about police matters. No word of the apartment, no hint, no glance of complicity ever passed between them; and if it hadn't been for the occasional flicker of compassion that Fred saw in Bob's brown dog eyes, he would have been able to forget that they were involved with each other in any way, or had any relationship except that which existed between a lieutenant and a detective attached to the same bureau.

He was therefore surprised when, coming off duty that evening and making his way—his direct way—back to his two rooms in Brooklyn, he found Bob waiting for him in the street, with the obvious intention of talking to him. He was surprised because he and Bob were working different hours at present, and because it had never happened before; but he was not angry, as he would have been at any other time. He couldn't be angry; he didn't have the strength. He was feeling too miserable, too confused, to be angry. He had been thinking about Smith all day, and he hadn't been able to concentrate on anything else. He hadn't even been able to play his part as a quiet, shy, neat man, which normally came so naturally he forgot it was only a part. Today he had spoken too loudly, and he had sworn at someone, and he had spilled some milk while having a snack he didn't want. Today he had felt like a whale stranded on a beach, left with only his size and the consciousness—now that he couldn't swim or send messages through the deep water in which he was used to living—of his size. He had been able to do nothing but think of Smith and ask himself, again and again, who he was and what he wanted. But he hadn't been able to think of any answers to his question. All he knew was that, whoever Smith was and whatever he wanted, he was the Enemy, and he was dangerous, and if he continued to haunt him in this way, something terrible would happen. Fred tried to tell himself again that Smith's desire to see him might be quite innocent. He even tried to tell himself that, since Smith knew he had the apartment, there was no point in keeping him out of the place itself, and that he would have done better to have him sent up—to face him, find out what it was he did want, and cope with the problem right away rather than flee from it and postpone it. But though he tried to tell himself all these things, he couldn't convince himself. He could only think that every moment he managed to put off that dreadful meeting was good for him, was to his advantage, and might even—if he could put it off long enough—give him time to think of some way to deal with it effectively, or to put it off forever.

As he saw Bob and murmured a prim and unfriendly "Hi" to him, he realized that not only was he not angry to see him, but he was in a way almost glad. For the first time, he thought he would quite welcome Bob's look of compassion.

But strangely, tonight, as Bob—with just a little too much gentleness—said, "Hi Fred. I'm sorry to waylay you like this, but I gotta speak to you," his eyes, which were normally so brown and understanding, staring directly into Fred's when he spoke to him, were lowered, and his expression was not so much one of concern for suffering humanity as it was very slightly sulky—one of concern for suffering Bob.

34

Fred nodded without saying a word, and continued to walk slowly down the street, waiting for Bob to fall in step with him and speak.

"I don't want to put you on the spot, Fred, but I've decided—I mean, I've been thinking about this for some time, but I really just decided today, and as I don't often see you —I mean I wanted to talk to you last night, but you left, and—well, look, Fred, I want to quit. I thought perhaps— you know, if you're okay for money—maybe you could buy out my half. I don't want to make any profit on it, and I'd sell for what we bought it for, but I sort of feel I'm betraying Lenore. It's like that place is another woman, and you know, if she ever found out—" He paused.

Fred stopped walking and turned to Bob; turned to look at his soft, handsome face and his lowered eyes, at his expression now of apprehension, and nodded. He didn't need to hear him say any more; didn't want to hear any more of that awkward, disjointed speech that was so unlike his normal, measured, reassuring bedside manner.

And then, again for the first time, he found himself adopting the tone of the friendly doctor. "That's okay," he muttered. "There's nothing to worry about. I got plenty of money. We'll go see a doc—" he checked himself and gave, surprisingly, a brief laugh—"I mean a lawyer, next week, and get it all settled. I understand. And you're right about Lenore. She really wouldn't like it if she found out. And you don't want to put your marriage in danger. Especially not with someone as great as Lenore." He stopped and looked down at Bob's lowered head and wondered for an instant whether he should pat him and say, "Good dog, go home now." Of course he didn't, but he did smile—without any effort at all—and say, "Just don't worry. I'll fix everything. And then you can just sign and it'll all be over. What you going to do with the money? Buy some place in the country?"

Bob, defeated now, shook his head. But then, obviously

making an effort and remembering that he wasn't alone in being a member of poor, wretched mankind, murmured, "No. I think I'll just give it away."

And now, unable to resist, Fred did pat him on the arm, and said, "Thanks for talking to me, Bob, and thanks for everything. You better be getting on home now."

Bob nodded. "See you around."

Fred stood still and watched him walk slowly, dejectedly away, and then called after him with a sort of laugh, "Watch out for the cop killer."

Bob turned and said, "I'll do that. And you watch out, too." And as he did so, he finally stared Fred right in the eyes and gave him what earlier Fred had half hoped to receive. He gave him—along with a look of unmistakable fear—a long gaze of the greatest, most profound pity that Fred had ever seen in his life.

That gaze stayed with him as he made his way to the subway, and as he waited on the platform. It stayed with him as he got on the Brooklyn express; it stayed with him as he thought that he should be happy, overjoyed, that Bob was finally leaving—and it stayed with him as he realized that he wasn't; when he realized that Bob's leaving him now was simply like a rat leaving a sinking ship. It stayed with him as he thought that rats were really very sharp animals, and as he realized that he was—or soon would be—alone at last, and that he was frightened.

It stayed with him as he got off the Brooklyn express at Boro Hall, and as he crossed the platform to change to the F train. And it only deserted him when, as he was about to get onto the waiting train, he saw, watching him, a slim youth wearing a black woolen cap and dark glasses. He knew the second he saw him, it was Smith.

He should have gone up to him, of course; talked to him, hit him, or arrested him. But, perhaps because of the shock of suddenly seeing him when he hadn't expected to, of suddenly realizing that he was more or less face to face with a figure who had become, in little over twenty-four hours, mythical; or perhaps for the same reasons he had given himself for not having Smith sent up to the apartment or going down to the lobby to meet him—i.e., that every second he avoided actually meeting the Enemy was time gained—he did none of these things, but simply turned, a vast red hippopotamus in a panic, and ran.

He bounded up the stairs of the subway, crashed through the exit barrier, and ran up the street. He ran as fast as he could, not really knowing where he was going, but knowing that he had to get away. He noticed the looks of surprise and fear on the faces of the people in the street; but, neat man that he was, he avoided bumping into anyone and didn't stop for a second. He ran, and found himself heading toward the Brooklyn Bridge, and after only a second's hesitation decided to let his body have its way and to cross it. Manhattan seemed more attractive than the quieter streets of Brooklyn.

But when he was on the bridge, with the cars, and the river beneath him, and the wind icy on his sweating face, he stopped running and started to walk. And then, panting, sweating, shivering, he even stopped walking. He was mad, he told himself. He should try to be calm. He closed his eyes for a second and repeated this to himself. He should try to be calm; he should go home, to bed. Yes. He should go home to bed. . . .

He turned—and then froze; froze as if the cold wind had suddenly iced his blood and paralyzed him. Because behind him, not fifty yards away, standing quite still and watching him through his black glasses, was Smith.

His first thought was that he would have liked to fling himself from the bridge and be drowned in the cold black water below. His second thought was that—he couldn't think.

He ran.

And now if anyone had been in his way he would have knocked them over, wouldn't even have seen them as he trampled them under foot. He ran faster, he was sure, than any man his size had ever run. He ran and ran and never looked around, and felt that if he did he would be lost forever, would be condemned for eternity to hell.

He didn't know how he kept running, how anyone could have kept running as long as he did. And when he thought he couldn't run any more, that his heart would explode, he only ran faster. He ran and ran and ran; he ran all the way to the City Hall subway station. And there he ran onto a train that arrived as he did. And only then, as he crashed into the car, amid the nervous and then averted glances of the other passengers—as if the sight of a terrified hippopotamus was not pleasant—did he stop. The doors closed behind him, and he sat down and started shaking and trying to control the vomit he felt rising within him. He shook and trembled and controlled himself for two stops, and then he could control himself no longer, and threw up. He vomited all over the floor of the car, and then he wiped his mouth with the back of his big red hand, stood up without raising his eyes—without daring to see the disapproval and disgust that he knew must surround him—and got off at the next stop.

He looked around only casually to make sure that Smith hadn't been on the train and gotten off too, didn't see him, and went up to the street.

He walked now, slowly and aimlessly, only waiting till he could feel something apart from the pain in his stomach, feet, legs, chest and head. He walked up and down, around and around, until he came to Washington Square; then he sat down on a bench and put his head between his hands, and told himself he wouldn't run again—not for anyone, not for any reason on earth.

He sat on the bench until he was too cold to sit there any longer; and then he walked until he found a bar, went in, and stayed there for an hour. He drank two whiskies. Then he went to another bar and drank two more. And then he went out into the street, feeling courageous once again, feeling proud of his size and strength, and feeling quite capable of dealing with Smith if he saw him now.

He didn't, however; or he didn't think he did. But then, New York was so full of shadows late at night, real and imaginary, that it was difficult to know who or what one saw. Especially when one was drunk. . . .

He went to three or four more bars, and walked around a great deal—looking, he told himself, for Smith—until three or four in the morning. Then he took a taxi back to Brooklyn.

At least when he woke the next morning, very late, he thought he had taken a taxi home. But he couldn't really remember. Maybe he had taken the subway. Or perhaps he had walked. Still, he seemed to remember taking a taxi somewhere, and he guessed it had brought him home. In any case, it didn't matter.

His sleeping late didn't matter either, since he wasn't working that day; so he took his time about getting up, shaving, showering, and taking a bus to the kiosk where, according to his diary, he had to buy his *Times*. It wasn't until two o'clock that afternoon that he got to the apartment on Central Park West and had a chance to read the paper—to read about, as the headline put it, "Another Policeman Murdered."

CHAPTER 3

According to the *Times*, there was some doubt as to whether the new murder was the work of "The Cop Killer." For one thing, the previous five murders had taken place at monthly intervals, whereas the killing last night had occurred only a few days after Officer Jim Parro's death. Secondly, Sergeant Petrie, the policeman killed last night, was not with the Narcotics Bureau, as the others all had been. Thirdly, he was stabbed to death with a smallish knife, whereas all the others had had their throats cut with a bread knife. And, lastly, the other murders had been distributed evenly around Manhattan: the first in Morningside Park, the second on East 70th Street, the third in Battery Park, the fourth on West 46th Street, and the fifth, the other day, on East 4th Street. One killing for each neighborhood. But the one last night had again been on the Lower East Side, on East 7th Street. It was too close to the previous murder. . . .

It was possible, of course, the *Times* said, that the Cop Killer was getting careless, in which case there was a hope that very soon he would make a slip and get caught. But it was far more likely that last night's murder had been an isolated, unconnected incident—either someone with a grudge against Sergeant Petrie who was trying to make it seem that his death was the work of the Cop Killer, or someone who just wanted to share in the Cop Killer's notoriety.

When Fred had finished reading about the killing he put the paper down on the floor. He guessed he should read the rest of it as he always did—just as he should have changed into his real clothes. But he didn't have the energy; he couldn't be bothered. All he felt capable of doing was waiting for the doorman to call up—in spite of his instructions—and tell him Smith was downstairs. He didn't even pour himself a glass of whiskey.

He just sat there, waiting. . . .

But though he sat there till six o'clock that evening, the doorman did not call up; and by the time Fred was ready to leave he was beginning to allow himself the hope that Smith had gotten tired of the game he was playing and wouldn't bother him any more. Then he even allowed himself to think of his talk with Bob the night before, and to be finally, unconditionally, glad about it. All this *would* be his, he thought, looking around. All this space would be his alone, and he would be able to take it all, at last, completely into himself; he would have this space, as it were, within his head, and he would be able to wander around in it without ever being afraid of bumping into any foreign bodies, of any germs infecting it. And perhaps he would not wait till he retired but would start to furnish it now, slowly, without any hurry, bit by bit, piece by piece, until finally the whole thing was a perfect, beautiful home—within himself. He closed his eyes and let himself soak in this dream for a moment or two. All this space, and the view . . . it was his soul. A great, wide, ordered soul, with a view. . . .

He went over to the window and stared out across the park to the lights on the East Side. All, all his . . .

He had sometimes wished that he and Bob had taken an

apartment on the East Side; after all, the East Side was traditionally the side that represented all that he admired and liked about New York, and the West Side definitely was not. But apart from the fact that it had been Bob who had found the apartment, and Bob had wanted to live on the West Side, he couldn't really regret it, mostly because—unless they had taken an apartment on Fifth Avenue or Central Park South, which might have been too expensive even for them—he would not have had a view of the park. And the park was important to him: that green rectangle with its twisting paths and lakes; that landscaped, lovely stretch of earth. It might no longer be the safe and perfect place that it had once been, and instead of merely representing nature, might have been allowed to return—in spirit if not yet in fact—to the wildness of nature itself, to anarchy and disorder and horror. But still, what it stood for—oh yes, that, almost as much as his apartment, was his soul. . . .

He sighed and came away from the window, wondering why Smith—Smith the Enemy, Smith the spirit of chaos—hadn't come today.

He didn't come the next day either, or the next; but the day after that, while Fred was in the subway making his way uptown to the apartment, he felt, or rather he knew, he was being watched. Quite how or from where, he didn't know, since he saw no one in the car he was sitting in who could have been Smith, even if he had taken off his dark glasses and his cap, or even if he had disguised himself in some way. There was simply no one of Smith's physical build. There was no one in the adjoining cars either, because he walked up and down the car he was in and looked into them. But he was being watched. He knew it.

When the train drew into the next station he waited

until everyone had gotten on, until he guessed the doors were about to close, and then he got off. As he did so, he was aware of a woman in the next car getting off, too. Was it a coincidence? he wondered. Had she almost forgotten her stop and then realized at the last moment? Or was she—no, she couldn't possibly be Smith. He noticed (out of the corner of his eye, because he didn't want to attract her attention if she had only forgotten to get off earlier) that she was small and somewhat plump. Even if Smith had decided to dress as a woman, he couldn't have shrunk ten inches or so. Besides, so far, Smith had made no attempt to disguise himself—unless dark glasses and a cap were a disguise—so it was unlikely that he would go to the length of changing sex in order to follow him. But as he lingered on the platform, wondering whether to go up to the street or simply wait for the next train and get on that, it occurred to him that Smith might not be alone. There might be two or three or even twenty Smiths, of all different sexes, ages, colors and shapes, following him. And this idea made him sweat even more than the idea of being followed by a single Smith did. More than one Smith could only mean that all these people were, like himself, policemen or women, and they were following him because they suspected him of—what? Of being corrupt, and of having an apartment on Central Park West that he couldn't have afforded on his lieutenant's pay? Hardly. They obviously knew already that he had an apartment on Central Park West, so if they had wanted to do something about that they could have done it by now. Not, surely, because they suspected he had anything to do with—or even was, himself—the Cop Killer. No. . . .

But as he stood there watching, still out of the corner of his eye, the small plump woman—who had wandered to the end of the platform but hadn't left it—he told himself that Smith, or the Smiths, couldn't be police. They were making no secret about following him, and yet they weren't approaching him either. But then who were they? What did they want, these one or two or more people who were pursuing him? More and more he felt himself to be helpless, lost and threatened by these unnamed—unnameable?—forces, as if they, like his apartment, were inside him and were eating like foul worms through his vital organs, even now gathering about his heart and brain, waiting for the final attack.

More people drifted onto the platform. He looked them over, wondering if there were any Smiths among them. But there was no way of knowing. Smiths looked the same as everyone else. Smiths *were* everyone else. He was becoming dizzy, with Smiths all around him, and Smiths within him. He thought he was going to faint. . . .

But then, through his faintness, he heard the rumble of an approaching train, and he managed to stand straight until it clattered into the station. This time, he thought, he would get in and wait till the doors were actually closing before he stepped off again. If he timed it right, that plump woman—he could see her edging down the platform toward him—*couldn't* get off behind him.

He did it beautifully, he thought; as neatly, cleanly, perfectly as if he had been trained in the movement for years. The doors just brushed his shoulders as he edged between them, back onto the platform. He stared down the train. No one else had gotten off. He grinned to himself and felt as elated as a small boy who has just successfully performed some daring and illegal deed. He watched the train as it pulled slowly out of the station, and then he turned, still grinning, to go up to the street. And then, as he turned, he stopped grinning and jumped. Because there, right in front of him, smiling at him, was the small plump woman. He closed his eyes and let the waves of chaos sweep him out to sea without so much as a struggle.

He was lost. And she, whoever she was, had won. Anticipating his move, she hadn't, he realized, gotten on the train at all.

"Are you okay, Fred?" he heard a harsh, bright, unsympathetic voice ask.

He opened his eyes and stared. Now, suddenly, he no longer saw the small plump girl as some nameless force of evil, some dark, threatening, symbolic figure, but as a real person whose face he hadn't even looked at properly. In spite of the fact that it had changed in the two years since he had last seen it, it was a face he recognized. He stared at the over-elaborate, rather old-fashioned and unflattering hair style, all stiff waves and curls; he stared at the body, really too plump to be encased in blue jeans and a tight sweater and an old fur coat; he stared at the gray eyes, at the small nose, at the red, sardonic mouth and the pale moustache above it, more noticeable now than it had been two years ago; and then, unexpectedly—extraordinarily for him—he laughed. It wasn't a pleasant laugh, he heard, or even a laugh of amusement; but he couldn't control himself. It was a laugh of terrible relief.

"Hi, Lenore," he said finally.

She narrowed her eyes, and her mouth twisted into the grim smile she always wore, he remembered, when she was moving in for an attack. It was the same smile she had worn when he had absurdly asked her, four and a half years ago, to marry him. . . .

"So," she cracked. "I'm hilarious. But do you have to run away from me when you see me? What the hell are you doing?"

Fred gazed down at her, and became serious. "I'm sorry," he said, "but I just didn't recognize you. I mean— I didn't see you."

"For Chrissake. I was standing next to you on the platform at Forty-second Street and you looked right at me."

45

"I'm sorry," Fred repeated.

"I thought maybe you hadn't recognized me or didn't want to see me. So I got in the next car. But then you came up and looked at me in there. So I thought, shit. And then when you got off I thought I'd get off, too, and speak to you, and then you looked right through me *again*. And then I thought I was being ridiculous, so I decided to let you get on this last train by yourself, and I'd wait for the one after. And now—you get right off again. I guess you thought I'd gotten on."

Fred nodded, and then said once again, "I'm sorry, Lenore. I just didn't recognize you. Your hair's different, and—I dunno. I just wasn't expecting to see you, and—I dunno. I mean you look—" He stopped. He was going to say, "You look like some old Jewish matron," but he guessed that was rude; what was more, it wasn't true, though it would be in a couple of years. He thought of her as she had been when he first met her, with her hair long and unstyled and just naturally wavy, and her body thin—well, slim anyway—and tiny.

Only the voice hadn't changed: that metallic, oh-so-aware and you-can't-fool-me voice, which was saying now, in the tones of a lady journalist doing her unsentimental and unflinching research into the quirks and aberrations of human nature, "Who the hell were you expecting to see?"

"I dunno," Fred muttered helplessly.

"Oh, for Chrissake. You were running away from me—or from whoever you thought I was."

"No," Fred said.

Lenore thrust her hands into the pocket of her ratty old fur and pulled out a pack of cigarettes. She took one and lit it, defiantly.

Feeling that it was expected of him, Fred murmured, "You can't smoke here."

Lenore paused long enough to thank him, with her eyes, for the opening he had given her, then glanced up and down the platform and said, "There are no cops about, except for you."

Fred stared at her.

"Where are you going then, if you won't tell me who you're running away from? Off to arrest someone? Or to rip someone off so you won't have to arrest them?"

"No," said Fred, "I'm not going anywhere."

Lenore laughed.

"How's Bob?"

"You're asking me? You work with him. You must see him more than I do."

"Yeah, I know. But I haven't seen him recently."

Lenore gazed at him thoughtfully now, and said, quietly, "Bob's scared of the Cop Killer."

Fred nodded.

"I don't like him going out by himself."

"Does he ever?"

"Go out by himself? Oh, sure." Lenore was still gazing at him. "Sometimes he goes out for long walks by himself. To think, he says. I told him he'll have to think with me from now on. Until they've caught the nut. If they ever do. *I* get scared when he's on duty though."

"He's never alone when he's on duty."

"I know, but—" The thoughtful gaze continued.

Fred, to make her stop, asked, "When did you get back?"

"This morning. How'd you know I'd been away?"

"Bob told me."

"I thought you hadn't seen him recently."

Oh, she was sharp. . . .

"I haven't. Not really. But I see him for a minute or two every now and then. He told me you were away. I asked after you."

47

"That was thoughtful of you, Fred."

Another train came into the station. Lenore asked, "Are you taking this one, or am I, or are we both?"

"You take it," Fred muttered, as if there were only one available place. "I think I'll walk for a while."

Once more the thoughtful gaze settled on him. "You're crazy," Lenore said, as pleasantly as she knew how. "You know that, don't you?"

Fred nodded.

"Okay then. Look after yourself, O'Connor."

Fred attempted a smile, and watched Lenore as she got onto the train. He waited for the doors to close.

They didn't.

Lenore was standing near them, and Fred asked, "Where are *you* going?"

Lenore laughed. "I'm going to have lunch with some old chums of mine who have just moved to New York. They've bought a grand apartment on Central Park West and want to show it off to me. Schmucks."

"What number?" Fred said—casually, but already guessing the reply.

"Eighty-eight. Why? Do you," Lenore mocked, "have some old chums at eighty-eight, by any chance?"

Fred was saved from having to answer by the doors at last closing. He just managed to say, "See you soon."

He saw Lenore murmur something and stare at him through the glass.

And then the train pulled out.

He walked up to the street. It was a gray and yellow day, and it was obviously going to snow again any second. But he hardly noticed the weather, or anything else. He felt too exhausted by his meeting with Lenore. So—she knew about the apartment. Bob had told her, or she had followed Bob. Or she really was going to have lunch with some old chums—how he hated the way she spoke!—who just happened to have an apartment in the same building as his. It would be a coincidence, of course, but Lenore was the sort of person who would have friends living there. Fashionable, liberal friends, who just adored Lenore, and would adore Bob when they met him, if they hadn't and didn't already. Bob's compassion would be great enough even for them, and they would say, without a hint of sarcasm in their voices, "He's a really fine, *good* person." Oh, yes, they would adore him and think him a saint, and their adoration would be completely genuine and uncondescending. Because, being Lenore's friends, they would be truly liberal. . . .

But he didn't care. If Lenore knew or not, it was all the same. He was too exhausted. Perhaps, he thought, if he ever did actually meet Smith he would find that he knew him too. Perhaps Smith was Lenore's brother. . . .

He raised his hand, stopped an empty cab, and told the driver to take him to Central Park West.

It was just a big empty apartment. That was all. There was nothing secret about it, nothing special about it. Everyone knew about it, and no one cared. It was Fred O'Connor's soul, and it was a big empty space. They probably laughed about it, and him, and his passion for it. They probably said to each other, "You can't even take Fred's corruption seriously. It's so innocent really. And so sad, and boring. At least if he took fancy girls out to fancy restaurants, or took fancy vacations, or bought fancy foreign cars— But, no, just a big, empty apartment. Poor Fred. Poor, poor Fred. . . ." Oh, he could hear them all say it.

And Lenore, he thought savagely as he sat hopelessly in his armchair, was their ringleader. Bright, smart Lenore with her harsh, smart voice and her moustache, who had always wanted to get her revenge on him for having once made love to her, for having dared to ask her to marry him, and possibly for having introduced her to Bob, whom she had married. Bright, smart Lenore, journalist and author of one critically praised but little bought novel, who had caught for an instant a glimpse of his dream—and who had, for an instant, been fascinated by it. And he, Fred thought, like a fool, had taken her fascination for approval; had taken it even as a longing to share in that dream. Wasn't she, after all, the literary lady, one of the great apostles of clear, classical writing? Wasn't she the great champion of editors, and editing, who believed that the book of life, as it were, could always be improved by a thorough purge of the careless, of the romantic, of the personal and subjective, so that what remained was the clear perfect image, the bright, diamond-hard object? She had told him so, at any rate, and he had believed her. But he had also believed that her vision wasn't limited only to the world of books. He had believed she was trying to tell him something more. Oh, what a fool he had been. He should have realized that she had discussed literature with him simply in the hope that he wouldn't understand what she was talking about, or simply as a hint that *his* vision—his romantic, personal, subjective vision—could do with some editing.

What a fool, what a fool he had been. Believing that Lenore's lovemaking had been serious, and not merely the literary lady, eager for experience, indulging her bestial curiosity, taking notes, he had trusted her. And being, according to his own lights, an honest man, a man of integrity, he had gone straight home and told Helen. And Helen—the good, kind, friendless Mrs. O'Connor—hadn't said a word; had simply, when he was working next day, packed her bags and left him. Soon after, he had gotten a letter from her lawyer, telling him that she was starting divorce proceedings. She hadn't wanted alimony; she hadn't wanted anything. She had simply decided that she couldn't remain married to an adulterer, someone who couldn't stick to the rules—rules which were, after all, the only thing that bound them together. Fred had considered going after her, going to beg her to come back to him. But he hadn't, partly because he knew she was right, one couldn't break the rules and hope to get away with it; and partly, mainly, because—despite his being upset by her departure and furiously angry with Lenore for having tricked him, betrayed him, humiliated him—he was glad to be alone; glad that nothing stood between him and his private life, his real life—his apartment.

Of course Lenore, when he told her what had happened, was properly contrite and apologetic, and even went so far as to suggest that she should go to Helen and say it was all her fault: that she, Moll Flanders of Greenwich Village, had seduced Mr. O'Connor, and had never *imagined* that her action would lead to anything as drastic as a separation or a divorce. But again, partly because he was basically glad to be alone, and partly because, decent as he was, he wanted to spare Helen from bright, treacherous Lenore—spare her the literary lady's *explanations,* and the lecture, such as she had given him, on how the breaking of the rules, just once, only made one more conscious of them; made one realize the importance of them; made one realize that compromise and acceptance and not some ideal was the true basis of a *real* relationship—he told her not to bother. Forbade her to, in fact.

He forbade her to; but up in the apartment, in the great panoramic space of his soul, he planned his revenge. And it had been almost too easy. Lenore's sharpness, wit and snappy intelligence were ultimately no match for his world-embracing vision, his perfectly trained instinct for the laws—the real laws—of nature. She was a snake, and she rejoiced in the fear and awe she inspired, and thought that her poison and her fangs made her superior to—and safer than—the other animals, who blundered past her in the sun while she lay, poised for striking those lovelier than she, in the shade so that her snake's blood would not boil: the snake's sole vulnerability. Yet she had a longing to forget her dangerous blood; a longing just to lie in the forbidden sun and be dumb as the other animals. She felt a great pity for herself because she couldn't. And this pity made her more vulnerable, made her weak and helpless before anyone who was able to see it and offer her the compassion she so deeply longed for; anyone who could feel sorry for her poison and her fangs and her condemnation to the shade.

And the one man who did have compassion enough for poisonous Lenore was, of course, Bob. And so, one day, he had introduced them. . . .

The beauty of this revenge was that it was double-edged. While Lenore would be rendered weak and vulnerable by the compassionate Bob, she would also hate him for the power he had over her; and while she was—as she had told Fred icily one day six months before her marriage—passionately in love with Bob, she would also, involuntarily, be searching for a chance to reassert her snake nature, and bite him. And she would find her chance, one day. Maybe she would find out about the apartment, or maybe something else would happen. But she would find it, and she would strike. And while Bob—as he had told Fred mournfully one day—was passionately in love with her, he knew this, and was frightened of her. Just as he was frightened of Fred, sorry for him though he was too, because he knew that Fred had in him the power to give Lenore the chance she was searching for.

Oh, it was perfect! Or at least it had seemed so when it all happened, just as he had planned it. But now, as he sat alone in his apartment, it no longer seemed so perfect. It no longer seemed perfect at all. It just seemed like an empty, silly game he had played—a game, what was more, that was going to backfire.

He put his head in his hands. It was all so clear now. Everything. Bob had told Lenore that Fred had the apartment, as a sort of safety measure so that if she ever found out he'd been going there—well, he could say that everyone went to visit poor Fred sometimes. And then Lenore had decided to write an article, about police corruption—or, better yet, about human folly, *Fred's* folly (his empty apartment, his life)—and had hired Smith to do some research for her, to get a look at the apartment if possible, maybe have a talk with "poor Fred." And when she had told Bob what she was doing, Bob had probably first tried to persuade her not to, and then, when that proved useless and he realized that his part in it might become known, he had asked Fred to buy him out, hoping that all the papers could be signed and dealt with before the article appeared—or before Fred suspected what was going on. That way there was only one owner of the apartment—Fred O'Connor—and there would be less danger that Lenore, or anyone else, would find out the truth. Fred was certain that Lenore wouldn't have told Bob about Smith. He would never have approved. That would have been too cruel. . . .

It was all so clear. . . .

But what could he do? Nothing. Nothing at all, he told himself. If he told Lenore about Bob now, that would only make her more savagely determined than ever to write her article. If he went to her and begged her not to—saying that since she had wrecked his marriage she might at least think twice about wrecking his life—she'd get all moral, as only the truly immoral can, and say that it was her duty to publish the truth. And if, as an extreme measure—and he considered the idea, though wildly—he killed Lenore, and Bob, and Smith, that would be useless, too. Because by now lots of people must know about the article, and to kill three people would only serve to put him in prison for life. It wouldn't be long before the reason for their deaths became obvious. No. If he was going to kill to prevent the article from being written, he would have to kill half New York. All those bright, guilty people who were destroying his dream. All those weak, evil people who knew about Fred O'Connor and were probably now, at this very minute, laughing at the big empty space that was his soul.

He sat there, hardly noticing that the snow had started to fall outside, hardly aware of his great red warrior's body, hardly aware of his quiet, beloved apartment. He sat there, really aware only of the fact that he had been defeated and there was nothing, nothing he could do about it. He sat there, only waiting, and wishing that the end would come quickly. He sat there and sat there—and when the doorbell rang he was almost happy that it was over. He got up quite lightly and easily to let Lenore in.

But when he opened the door he didn't see Lenore. He saw only a youth in a black woolen cap and dark glasses. He saw, in fact, only Smith. Still, he wasn't particularly surprised. He guessed that it didn't make any difference.

He said, "Where's Lenore?"

The youth pulled off his cap—he had longish pale hair—and frowned. "Who's Lenore?" he asked. He had a thin, weak voice.

Fred shrugged. He was too tired to play games. He murmured, "You coming in?"

The youth nodded, took two steps forward, and took off his dark glasses. He had pale, watery blue eyes that were red around the rims. He said, "Hi, I'm Leo Smith."

Wearily, Fred said, "Hi." Then, "How come the doorman didn't call up?"

The youth giggled. "There was only one on duty, and I waited until he was helping some old lady into a taxi. Then I slipped in."

Wearily, Fred nodded. It didn't matter how he had come in. Nothing mattered any more. He said, "Did Lenore—" and then he stopped. The phone was ringing. Not the house phone, but the regular phone. Only he and Bob had the number.

The youth started, "Who's this Len—" but Fred held up his hand to silence him.

After two rings the phone stopped. It was Bob's signal. Although only the two of them had the number, they had agreed always to give two rings, hang up, and then ring again, when they wanted to call each other. Fred wondered whether he should answer, when Bob called back. After all, what could Bob say now? But then, when the phone started ringing again, he thought that he might as well. Maybe Bob would have some plan for stopping Lenore and Smith. He picked up the phone—it was on the floor by the door—and said, "Hi, Bob?"

"Yes, it's me," Bob said sadly. "You haven't seen Lenore, have you?"

"No. But—"

"Thank God," Bob interrupted, sounding strangely excited now—at least for him. "I just got in and there's a note from her here. She said she's gone to have lunch with some old friends of hers who've just moved back to New York. And guess where they live! Eighty-eight Central Park West! It's incredible! I couldn't believe it when I saw it. I imagined you bumping into each other in the elevator." He laughed nervously. "It must be the apartment above ours. The doorman told me that some new people were moving in a couple of weeks ago. Anyway, Lenore left me the telephone number, and it's not ours!" Another laugh. "But be careful when you're leaving."

"I will," Fred said, "and thanks for letting me know."
He sounded, and felt, friendlier toward Bob than he had
felt since that first day in the shabby bar on Avenue B.
"That's quite a coincidence, isn't it?" he added.

"It sure is." Bob laughed once more. "I hope she doesn't
go to visit these friends too often. Otherwise—"

"Bob," Fred said, "I'm taking a shower. I'll see you later.
But thanks again."

"You're welcome," Bob said. "See you."

Fred hung up, took a step over to the door, and put the
chain on it. And then he started laughing, much as he had
done when he recognized Lenore in the subway. Only this
time he didn't stop immediately. He laughed and laughed
and laughed, and as he laughed he felt all his power and
sense of safety returning to him. Well—almost all his sense
of safety. There was still this Smith to be dealt with. But
now that he knew that there was no organized plot against
him, that not everyone knew about his apartment, and
that everyone wasn't laughing at him and planning to destroy him, he felt he could deal with anything. He laughed
and laughed and laughed; at least two minutes passed before he was able to control himself and turn to face the
pale, red-eyed youth who called himself Smith.

Towering over him, Fred growled, "Who the hell are
you?"

Smith lowered his eyes for a second and gave a slight
smile. Then, looking up again with a coy expression and a
coyer little shrug of his shoulders, he murmured, "I'm the
Cop Killer."

CHAPTER 4

Fred stared at the youth, stared at him as if he would crush him with his eyes. He took in the pale weak face, the pale thin hair, the white thin hands—hands so thin they looked like a monkey's—and the pale lips, now no longer smiling, but trembling slightly. With fear? With excitement? He didn't know. He looked at the shabby brown suede jacket, the high-necked black sweater, the jeans and the heavy shoes, which were stained with damp and had a ring of white around them where the salt on the snowy sidewalks had eaten into them. He wondered how old Smith was. Twenty-two? Thirty-two? It was difficult to tell in one so pale and weak. He must have looked the same at fourteen, and he would look the same at forty. Fred stared at him and stared at him, and then, remembering how he had run from this wretched, weak creature, how this pale thin figure had pursued him and frightened him, he suddenly lost control of himself. He lifted one of his great hands and hit the youth across the side of the face; hit him so hard that Smith fell to the floor, and blood started running from his nose. He wanted to kick him then, kick him in the face, in the stomach, in the kidneys, in the groin; and he would have if the pale watery blue eyes hadn't gazed up from the floor and—there was no doubt about it—willed him to do just that, begged him silently to do it—to kick him, beat him, smash him to pieces.

He stood over the wretched, bleeding figure and then took a step back; and then, suddenly, he said, "I've seen you before somewhere."

"We saw each other in the subway. And on Brooklyn Bridge," Smith murmured pleasantly in his soft monotone. He sounded as if he were at a cocktail party, smooth and languid and social. He was from New England, Fred guessed.

"No. I've seen you somewhere else—without all your gear on."

Smith smiled. "You might have. I mean I've seen you. Lots of times." Then he frowned. "Oh, I know. It was at a newsstand on Forty-second Street. Outside the public library. You were trying to buy the *Times*. They didn't have it. That was the first time you ever actually looked at me, I think."

Fred remembered that morning; and he remembered the pale thin youth who had been standing there, and who had disappeared when he had to ask a second time for the paper. Was this the same person? He stared. It was possible. And then he remembered having thought that the youth was no one to worry about. Yes. He guessed it was the same. Though really, with a face like that it was difficult to be sure. There were so many weak, wretched faces in New York.

Smith wiped his bleeding nose with the back of his hand and murmured, in his same social manner, "Do you think I could get up? Otherwise I'm going to spill blood all over your carpet."

"Yeah," said Fred and watched the youth—well, he guessed he was still just a boy, however old he was—pick himself up.

"Do you have a handkerchief?"

Fred felt in his pocket and handed him one, and then suddenly thought that he'd better frisk the boy and make sure he wasn't armed.

Holding the handkerchief to his nose with one hand, his other hand held theatrically vertical, Smith didn't protest or say a word till Fred had finished; then, pleasantly as ever and with a soft flat laugh, he said, "I left my bread knife at home."

Fred made himself stop to think before he said any more—made himself think what he *could* say, or do, with this feeble creature who said he was the Cop Killer.

"Why've you been following me?" he finally managed.

"Oh, I was just very tired suddenly," Smith breathed wearily, as if three sets of tennis were really too much for him. . . .

"So—?"

"So I thought I'd give myself up." He smiled again.

It wasn't tennis he'd been playing, but hide-and-seek. . . .

"And why'd you choose me?"

Smith gazed at him with his red-rimmed eyes and finally stopped smiling. "I had to give myself up to someone. But I didn't want to go up to just any cop and say, 'I'm the Cop Killer.' I had to choose. And I thought you were—the best."

"Why?" Fred repeated.

Smith glanced around the empty hallway and down the long corridor. It was the glance of someone who was used to big apartments. "Well," he said, "it had to be someone special. Someone who would understand."

"How long have you been following me?"

"About a year, I guess." Smith frowned. "I can't really remember the exact date. But—about a year."

Fred hit him again. It was almost involuntary. He couldn't stand that face and that voice. The blow sent Smith staggering back across the hall, but he didn't fall over; nor did he even put his hand to his face, which was red now, and bruised. In fact he didn't seem to be aware that he'd been hit at all. He went on, "I guess that was another reason why I finally let you see me. I was getting bored with following you. Bored with everything." He narrowed his eyes. "That's why I killed that last cop—Petrie—in a different way. I just couldn't be *bothered*. And the papers were right. I was getting careless, and if I'd gone on I probably would have been caught." He shrugged, thoughtfully. "I guess I shouldn't have killed him at all. I mean it was sort of messy, and spoiled the style of all the rest. But then it was also a sort of joke. You know—just to confuse everyone."

Fred—mighty, and red—looked down at the pale, bleeding boy. He said quietly, "You're not the Cop Killer. You never killed anyone in your life. You're just some sick creep who—" Who what? He didn't know. He stopped.

"You're right in a way," Smith agreed affably. "*I* never have killed anyone. I mean—*I* never have."

Fred stared.

"But sometimes—" Smith laughed coyly—"I'm not I. Me. I mean—I never really knew what I was doing when I went after those guys. I mean I planned everything very carefully, and I chose all men from the same division, and I always did it in the same way—apart from this last one—so everything would be neat and, like I said, stylish. But I've got another life, a regular life—" He smiled. "I live with my grandmother mostly, in Providence. She's rich and she'll leave me all her money when she dies. At least I lived mostly with her until about a year ago. When I found you. Since then, instead of just coming down to New York for two or three days a week, I've been down here nearly all the time. I've just been going up to Providence for the day, every now and then. But that's my real life, if you like. All this thing with the cops—that's just been my secret life, sort of." He glanced again around the hallway and down the corridor. "But it was a secret life I couldn't admit even to myself. In a way it wasn't me who was killing those cops. You see—I knew exactly what I was doing, but—I didn't know what *I* was doing, if you follow. It was like I was dreaming that I was awake. I knew I wasn't awake, but I behaved in my dream exactly as if I were. And that's another reason why I had to stop. Because the dream and the real life were growing farther and farther apart, and I could see the day coming—" he sounded quite indignant now—"when I didn't have any real life left at all. Only the dream. I—"

"Bullshit," Fred said.

"Excuse me?"

"Bullshit, I said. That's all bullshit."

Smith shrugged, unoffended. "Well it might be, but it's true too."

"And what's this now, here with me? You, or not you?"

Smith smiled. "Oh, this is me. I mean eventually I *had* to admit to myself what I'd been doing. After all," he went on casually, and with the air of explaining something simple to a cretinous child, "we are responsible for our dreams, aren't we? Just as much as we're responsible for our reality, let's say."

"For Chrissa—"

But Smith hadn't finished. "And like I said, that's the reason why I chose you to come to. Because if I'd just gone up to any old cop and said 'I'm the Cop Killer'— well—I couldn't have admitted it. Because it *wasn't* me, so I couldn't have admitted it. I've never, even for a second, admitted it to myself until this minute. But somehow I knew you'd understand me." He gazed at Fred almost flirtatiously now. "I mean, I didn't know what this place of yours would be like. I thought it might be all full of priceless antiques, or full of paintings of nude women, or— anything. But I knew that whatever it was like, and whatever you were like, you were the right person to come to."

Bullshit, Fred wanted to say again. But he didn't. Instead he muttered, "How did you know?"

"Well, I had to follow and check up on a lot of cops. I mean—you know—to pick my victims. But the very first time I followed you—" he smiled—"you went all the way uptown on the East Side to buy the *Times,* and then went all the way back downtown, and then came all the way back up here, and I knew. I knew. I mean—I knew," he repeated.

Weakly now, Fred said again, "You're not the Cop Killer. You're just crazy."

Smith paused before replying, and looked down at his thin pale hands. Then he looked up again and raised his eyebrows. "Well, you might be right," he said. "About my not being the Cop Killer. I mean, I explained—" Then he stopped, and obviously changed his mind about what he was going to say. "But I say I am. And that means—well, you can't just throw me out, can you? Because you never know. I might never have another moment of sanity, therefore might go on killing for the rest of my life. So you've got to arrest me, don't you? Unless—" he paused once more, and yet again seemed coy, flirtatious—"you kill me. In which case, if I am the Cop Killer, that's the end of that. And if I'm not, well, at least I'll never be able to tell anyone—your superiors, or the press—about all this."

"If," Fred said slowly, "I do arrest you, will you—" he cleared his throat—"tell anyone about me? About this?"

Smith smiled. "Well, I might and I might not. But you can't count on my word. After all, as you said, I'm crazy."

Fred's throat was dry. He couldn't think. He said, even more slowly, and hearing the lunacy of his words, "Do you want me to kill you?"

But if he was feeling out of his depth, Smith seemed to be full of confidence, even enjoying himself. "Well," he purred smoothly, "it would be the ultimate experience, wouldn't it? Like the dream and reality becoming one in death."

He sounded as if he were proposing a new game to his rich Rhode Island friends; and Fred, helpless now, whispered, "How do you—I mean, would you—want me to kill you?"

"Oh, I don't know," Smith sighed, as if unable to choose among a hundred different dishes on a menu. "Slowly, I guess. Just so I *would* experience it. *Really.*"

Fred closed his eyes and floundered, struggled in the waters that were engulfing him. And then suddenly, without quite knowing how, he found himself shooting to the surface, breaking out into the air. Suddenly he could see clearly again, could breathe. Smith *was* crazy, and he was here in his apartment; but outside it was a gray, snowy February day, and people were going about their business, and he himself—he looked at his watch—had to go on duty quite soon. Smith was a problem, a terrible problem; but like any problem, he could be dealt with as long as Fred thought about him rationally and logically. What was he? A crazy youth who said he was the Cop Killer. What was to be done about him? Fred didn't know, but certainly nothing rash. He would think about it and decide.

The firm policeman with the neat mind said, "I don't know what I'll do about you. But I gotta go to work now. I'll come back later this evening."

"That's okay. I'll wait," Smith murmured airily.

Fred finally permitted himself one of his smiles. "You better believe you'll wait. I'm going to make damn sure you wait."

"Are you going to tie me up?" The boy sounded eager now—and he looked as eager as he had when Fred had hit him, and when he had suggested that Fred kill him.

His eagerness made Fred feel sick; but he said, "Yes."

"How long will you be away?"

"I'll be back around ten this evening, I guess."

"What happens—" the voice was plaintive, but also very slightly amused—"if I have to pee?"

Fred considered for a moment; then he said, "I'll tie you up and lock you in the bathroom."

Smith nodded approvingly, as if he had already foreseen that move.

"What are you going to tie me up with?"

Fred considered again; then he muttered, unwillingly, "A tie, I guess."

He did tie the boy up with a tie—or rather, with two ties. Two of his fine silk ties. It made him mad to do it, but there was no alternative. Before he tied him up, however, he made him strip: first, because he thought that, without clothes, the boy couldn't get away even if he managed to untie himself; and secondly, so that if Smith did, as he said, want to pee, at least he'd be able to.

The boy naked was even more weak and thin than he had seemed dressed, and his skin was white and very dry and flaky. Fred tried to avoid touching him as he tied him up; when he did, unavoidably, once or twice, the feel of that dry flaky skin made him shiver with disgust. He tied the hands very securely in front of the boy; the feet he left slightly freer. When he had finished, he filled up the washbasin with cold water.

He said, "You can drink if you want to, and you can pee to your heart's content."

Smith nodded. "Fine. I'll see you around ten then."

"Yeah," Fred said.

He locked the bathroom door from the outside, put the key in his pocket, and put the boy's clothes in a closet.

Then, carefully, remembering that Lenore was somewhere in the building, he left the apartment.

During the day, he realized he had to decide two things. One was what he already knew he had to decide—i.e., what to do about Smith. The second only occurred to him as he was walking down the street, away from the apartment, and the second problem was what to do about Bob. He guessed that Bob wouldn't go to the apartment any more, now that he had finally decided to quit their partnership. On the other hand, he just might, if not today (since he had been on duty last night), then tomorrow sometime. And if he discovered Smith there, what would he do?

It was a difficult problem, and throughout the day Fred tossed and turned the advantages and disadvantages of telling him about Smith and asking his advice, or not telling him anything and dealing with Smith himself.

By six o'clock that evening he still hadn't decided what to do about Bob, so he put the matter aside temporarily and turned his attention exclusively to the problem of Smith.

He thought about Smith as logically and rationally as he had told himself he must, and by the time he came off duty he had more or less made up his mind.

Earlier, he had been taken off balance by Smith's craziness and his seeming eagerness to be killed. The idea had seemed monstrous to him, and insane. But now, being quite cold and objective about it, he saw that killing Smith was, in fact, the only solution—unless he wanted to run the risk of losing his apartment, his job and everything he lived for. He was equally clear about how he would kill him. That night, late, he would untie the boy, dress him, and get him out of the building without the doorman seeing them. Then he would walk him a few blocks uptown, maybe to the park behind the Museum of Natural History. Then, making sure that no one was about or able to see them, he would cut himself with his bread knife (which he would have brought from the apartment), slightly—on the hand, or arm, or somewhere. And then he would shoot Smith. He would quickly put the boy's dead hand on the handle of the bread knife, and then call for help. He would say he had been going uptown for some reason after he had come off duty, and had realized when he was in the subway that he was being followed. He had gotten off the train at 81st Street, suspecting by then who his follower might be, and thinking to lead him into a trap. He had wandered around for a while, and then had gone into the park behind the natural history museum. And there he had suddenly lost sight of his pursuer, who was nothing if not clever, and he had very nearly been caught in his own trap. Because after he had concluded that maybe he had been mistaken after all, he had decided to go home. But he was just walking out of the park when this guy had suddenly jumped out from behind a tree with a knife in his hand. He was still half expecting, half prepared for an attack, so he was quick enough to lift an arm to defend himself. The knife had cut his arm, but he had managed to grab his gun. And then—he had shot him.

And that would be that. He would be a hero, the papers would have their Cop Killer, and his apartment, his life, would be safe. The only thing that could go wrong would be if someone saw him walking Smith up to the museum and remembered him when his photo was in the papers. But with any luck it would still be snowing tonight, and there wouldn't be too many people in the street. Those

66

there were, he and Smith could hide from in doorways—
they would walk up Columbus Avenue rather than Central Park West, which had few if any unattended doorways—and that way, anyone who was aware of them
would hurry past, or even cross the street, thinking the lurk-
ing figures were muggers waiting for a victim.

He would gag Smith and put a scarf over his mouth in
case he tried to say anything or shout for help—though
somehow, frighteningly, he didn't think that Smith would
say anything, or shout for help. Rather, he would silently,
slimily, gleefully, take part in the game—right up to the
very end. . . .

He was feeling so calm that night, so sure of himself as
he came out of the blessedly heavy, driving snow into the
warmth of his lobby, that he knew nothing would, or
could, go wrong. Already the problem of Smith, like a leak-
ing faucet that a plumber was on his way to fix, was fading
from his mind. The whole matter was resolved, apart from
a few messy particulars, and already he was beginning to
look ahead and anticipate with pleasure the post-Smith
and post-Bob period of his life—when he would be threatened from neither within nor without, and when his apartment would be secret again and entirely his. Maybe, he
told himself as he took the elevator up, Smith was a sort of
final initiation rite he had to undergo before he could be
judged pure enough and strong enough to enter into full
possession of his kingdom of heaven. And, he told himself,
he *was* pure and strong enough. There was no doubt in his
mind at all. He even welcomed this final trial.

But, when he went into the apartment, the one thing
that he had discounted as most unlikely, and which he

would have so terribly feared if he had considered it a real possibility, had happened. Bob had come to the apartment. He was sitting in the living room, his handsome face absolutely racked, transfigured with pity, listening to a white, flaky, naked Smith, a Smith with a bruised face and a superior, sickening smile, tell him how he had killed six cops.

Fred took the whole scene in at a glance, and didn't allow himself even a moment of panic or despair at seeing all his perfect plans vanish into thin air; he couldn't: he had to keep all his wits about him for this new, unexpected and dreadful turn of events.

He stood massively in the door of the room and said primly to Bob, "I wasn't expecting to see you."

"I—" Bob cleared his throat; he was obviously so overcome with emotion at this chance of playing, at last, Jesus himself that he could hardly speak. "I thought I'd come and pick up my things before I went on duty. You know—now that Lenore's back, and especially since she's got these friends here—I thought this would be the last time. And now—Christ, Fred, what are we going to do?"

Fred noted, with just a grain of satisfaction, that Bob at least had the sense to see that there was a problem here, and wasn't (yet, at any rate) prepared to play Jesus to the extent of sacrificing himself, his marriage, his job and his almost ex-partner by turning Smith in. He even wondered briefly whether the pity in Bob's face was for Smith or for himself. A bit of both, he guessed.

"How the hell do I know?" he muttered, careful not to look at Smith, in case he should see some sign of joy at the fix in which he had placed his captor. "I've been thinking all day. How did you get into the bathroom?"

"I saw that there was a light on in there, and heard someone moving about. I thought it was you. So I asked, and then—all the keys in all the bathrooms are the same."

Fred nodded. It had been a ridiculous question, and he wasn't remotely interested in Bob's answer. It didn't matter how he had found Smith. The fact was, he had. And that was that. He looked down at his seated partner and murmured, "It's time for you to go, Bob. I'll deal with this."

Obediently, Bob stood up; but he said, "How?"

Fred made a motion with his head, toward the corridor. Bob walked past him, frowning, and waited until Fred had closed the door of the living room, locked it behind him, and ordered him into the kitchen.

He went.

"First of all," Fred said, "that kid isn't the Cop Killer. He's never killed anyone in his life. Unless—" he paused— "maybe that last one, Petrie, was his. Maybe he killed once and now feels so guilty he wants to confess to the lot. Or maybe he wants some sort of sick glory. I don't know. But I'm pretty sure he's never killed anyone. He's just some sort of nut. A freak. And he found out about this place and, I dunno. I mean—he's crazy. But he's not the Cop Killer. I'm sure of that."

"How can you be sure?" Bob asked, almost wistfully. He wanted Smith to be the killer, Fred guessed, so that he could have, at last, an object worthy of his compassion.

"I feel it. And if he's not the Cop Killer, I'm not taking him in so he can tell the world about—all this. And you can't want him to, either."

Bob dolefully shook his head.

"What's more," Fred continued, "even if he were—which he's not—the killer, I still don't see why we should lose all this."

Bob merely nodded.

"So first I gotta find out exactly who he is and what he wants, and second, think what to do about him—without getting us involved."

"But how—?"

Fred looked into Bob's eyes, into his sad brown cow eyes, and wondered whether he would stand for murder. Probably he would, he thought. But if he did, it would only mean putting himself more completely in Bob's power. Bob's knowledge of the apartment in the future, when he was no longer a partner, would be bad enough; but if Bob knew him to be a murderer as well, Fred would be his prisoner forever. A prisoner of pity . . . No. He couldn't kill Smith. Not any more. There was also the possibility that Bob *wouldn't* stand for murder. He would do nothing to prevent it, and might even, dumbly, weeping invisibly for the sorrows of the world, encourage it. But then when it was done he might just tell the whole story. Oh, no. He couldn't trust Bob.

Fred said, "I'll find some way. Don't you worry."

Bob stood there, still frowning, looking at the floor, clearly thinking along the same lines as Fred himself. But, just as clearly, he wasn't going to commit himself, even with a glance, to any course of action which he might later regret—or of which he might later be accused by Fred of having approved. His stance and frown seemed to say that he would allow Fred to take any action he thought right, and then he and his conscience would deal with that action as they thought right. He had been presented with the favorite gift of the sanctimonious, a moral dilemma, and by God he was going to follow it through to the end, even if—especially if?—it meant he would end up being crucified and torturing himself for his refusal to take a stand when he could have, when he should have.

"Okay," he murmured.

He didn't meet Fred's eyes again, not even for a second, until he left the apartment. But he was so obviously sighing within, wanting Fred and the weeping angels to be aware of his anguish, that Fred, in spite of himself, couldn't help saying again, "Don't you worry," even while he felt that he had never despised anyone as much as he despised Bob at that moment.

As soon as he had closed the door behind Bob, however, Fred put him out of his mind and forced himself to concentrate on Smith again, and on what he ought to do about him. He thought perhaps the best thing would be to ask the boy himself, since he seemed, after all, the person most eager to have his fate settled.

When he unlocked the door of the living room, Smith, who was sitting in one of the armchairs, gave a little smile. "I'm sorry," he drawled. "That was a mistake."

Fred said nothing.

"I didn't know about him. I mean—I thought this place was all yours."

"It is."

"I couldn't believe it when he opened the door of the bathroom."

Fred still said nothing, but when Smith curled his upper lip in an expression of disdain and murmured, "Who *is* he?" Fred did feel, for the first time, that the boy wasn't completely mad.

"When I bought this place I didn't have enough money to go into it by myself," Fred said. He didn't want to tell Smith that the apartment had been Bob's idea; that without Bob neither he nor Smith would be here now.

"This sort of changes everything," Smith said, sounding disappointed now, and dejected.

"He won't do anything."

Smith shrugged and pouted. "It still changes everything. Doesn't it?"

"I don't know. I guess so," Fred said, trying to sound more confident and aggressive than he felt.

He started pacing awkwardly up and down the room, ill at ease.

71

"Perhaps," Smith said, "you'd better just give me back my clothes and let me go."

Fred stopped pacing. "You're not going anywhere."

The boy looked thoughtful. "You're *sure* he won't do anything, or say anything?"

"Not yet," Fred said. He now shrugged. "Did you tell him how you got here?"

"I told him I saw you and I knew you were the right person to confess to." Smith smiled. "He said he understood."

"I bet."

"He did."

"Yeah. I bet he did," Fred repeated bitterly. "I believe you."

There was a moment's silence; then Smith, pouting again, whined, "*Fuck*. You might have told me."

"I didn't think he would show up here. I'm buying out his share of the place."

"I just never expected it of you."

Fred sat down in the other chair and looked at the bare wall of the room. "What do you suggest?"

"I don't know. I think if everything *has* changed, you should let me go. But otherwise—if you really think your friend won't do anything, or say anything—then you should do what you would have done if he hadn't shown up."

"I was planning," Fred said quietly, "on killing you."

As he said it, the light in the room seemed to dim slightly, and he became aware of the silence of the apart-'ment, and the snow-muffled sounds of the outside world. The apartment had never seemed more secret.

Smith obviously felt it too, because he became tense suddenly, and seemed once again, as he had that morning, to be enjoying himself; to be, in his puny, wretched way, willing Fred to do something dreadful.

"How?" he whispered eagerly.

Fred told him.

When he had finished, Smith said, "You'd have to make sure no one saw us walking up to the museum together."

"Yeah, I know."

"And you'd have to make sure I didn't run away."

"Would you?" Fred said softly, feeling slightly shocked.

"Sure. I might. I mean there'd be no fun if I just trotted uptown after you, would there? I mean—that'd be no game at all."

Fred closed his eyes. The boy was right. It was a game. A mad, sick game. But it was a game on which his life depended. Almost whispering now, the apartment getting quieter and quieter, more and more secret, he said, "I could keep a gun in your back. Then if you tried to get away I'd shoot you and say that I had arrested you on suspicion, and—"

"If you arrested me, why'd you be walking me uptown in a snowstorm? Why wouldn't you be calling in for help, for a car to come and pick me up? And anyway, I might not run. I might just call for help. Say something to someone. Say you were a nut."

"Apart from the fact that I'd gag you and put a scarf over your mouth, even if you did manage to say something, no one would take any notice of you. They'd think you were crazy. They'd run away from you. And if I did shoot you, I probably wouldn't stop to explain. I'd run away as fast as hell. No one would follow me. Not if I was armed. We could leave here by taking the service elevator down, and go out through the service door in the basement. I can open that. That way the doorman wouldn't see us leave. And I could come back the same way. No one would have seen me leave or come back."

Fred felt himself trembling as he imagined riding the service elevator down to the gray, silent basement, taking care in case there was someone around—someone checking on the furnaces, or doing something in the superintendent's office—and then opening the door and slipping out with Smith into the dark, white, freezing night. . . .

"Someone might recognize you on the street," Smith whispered, "even if they didn't try to stop you."

"I'd wear your cap," Fred whispered back. "And your dark glasses maybe. No one would recognize me."

Smith too was trembling; Fred could see him. Then the boy stood up and went over to the door and turned out the lights in the room so that he was only a pale, ghostly figure, just visible in the slight glow that the streetlights, far below, reflected into the room through the falling snow.

"Shall we try it?" he breathed. "I can't promise you I won't do anything unexpected. I mean—you can't have it all your own way. But, well, we've both got a chance. And—"

Fred closed his eyes. It was a game. An evil, insane game. And yet—

"No," he said, "I can't trust Bob. I can't risk it. Even if everything went all right, when you were found dead—"

"He can't do anything. He's involved."

"He might do something anyway. I can't risk it."

"He won't. Not when it comes to it. If you present him with the fact. After all, why should he? At that point he's got everything to lose by saying something, and nothing to gain."

"He might anyway. You don't know him."

"Oh, I think I do," Smith breathed mysteriously. "I'm a great expert on human nature. But anyway—so it's a risk. Well? You've got to take risks. There's no game in the world without a risk. And then, just think—with me dead, you'd be safe. I mean really, completely safe. With me alive, you can't be sure."

Fred listened to the boy, pale in the doorway, tempting him. He listened to the boy's heavy breathing, and to his own. He imagined the scene, and he imagined Smith's

74

blood spreading out in the snow. Perhaps, he thought, rather than go through all that business in the park, with the knife, and all the explanations that would follow, he would just shoot the boy in the street, as soon as he was sure there was no one around, and run. Yes. That would be much better. And, also, that way Smith would be taken off guard. If he were planning to make some move, do something to make the game more exciting, he would probably do it when they got to the park. But if they never did get to the park . . . Oh, yes. And then he would come back, and his apartment would be safe again, and Bob— well, as Smith said, he would just have to risk Bob.

He listened to his breathing and felt his mouth dry with excitement. He felt his heart pumping blood through his big body. He told himself that it was madness; absolute, total madness.

He stood up and crossed the room and walked past Smith.

"Come on," he whispered. "Your clothes are in the closet."

They were ready. He had tied Smith's hands behind his back, put a sock in his mouth, and wrapped his cashmere scarf around his neck and chin. He had the boy's cap pulled down over his own head, right down to his eyes. As soon as they were in the street he would put on the dark glasses too. He had his gun ready in his pocket. Everything was ready. He nodded at Smith, and Smith, whose red-rimmed eyes were glistening and running, nodded back. They walked together toward the door. . . .

And then the phone rang. It rang twice and then stopped. Smith shook his head violently and made sounds through the sock in his mouth, which Fred knew meant "Don't answer."

But he had to. What if Bob had turned the gift of his

moral dilemma around in his hands a bit and decided that after all he didn't really like it, or want it? What if Bob had already told someone? What if Bob—the phone started to ring again, and he bent down to pick it up.

Smith leaped at him and almost knocked him over. He kicked at Fred and tried to push him away from the phone. He tried to butt him with his head. He tried to stand over the phone and make it impossible for Fred to pick it up. But Smith's hands were tied behind his back, and he was thin, and weak. Fred hit him once, quite hard, and then, as the boy collapsed on the floor, his eyes not just running now but actually weeping—with fury? with pain?— Fred lifted the receiver. "Bob?"

"Yes. Listen, Fred—you haven't done anything to that boy?"

"No. Of course I haven't." Fred heard himself panting, and his voice was thick. He wondered whether he should try to explain why to Bob. He decided not to.

"Thank Christ," Bob said. "Because, listen, Fred. I know you're not going to like this, but I think—in spite of every-thing—and I know what this means—we should hand the boy over."

CHAPTER 5

The game was over. Or, to be more exact, since it had never actually started, the game was off. That was the first thing Fred realized as he heard Bob's words. The second thing he realized was that, while he despised Bob even more for chickening out, for returning the gift almost unopened, he was also very relieved. The plan would never have worked. It never could have worked; in fact, he himself might not have been able to see it through, might have chickened out. The third thing he realized was that he should never have allowed Smith to tempt him into it. And the last thing he realized was that if he didn't persuade Bob to change his mind, he was doomed.

His voice was quite clear now, though very prim. "I sort of agree with you, Bob. I've been thinking about this myself. But we've got to find a way of handing him over without this place getting—you know. In fact I think I've found a way. But I must talk to you about it. Can we meet tomorrow morning?"

He said it, he thought, magnificently. There was no doubt in his voice, no hesitation. There was only the tone of a calm, reasonable person suggesting something reasonable.

Bob's relief, when he spoke, was as pronounced as Fred's own; he allowed himself to sigh aloud now. "Thank God," he said. And then, to justify his concern: "I was worried about you, Fred. I know how much the apartment means to you, and what a shock this must have been. I was scared you might do something—wild."

How kind of you, Fred thought. He said, "I'll see you at eight tomorrow morning then."

"Where? At the apartment?"

"No," Fred said firmly. He didn't want Bob coming to the apartment any more. Okay, he couldn't kill Smith, but whatever he did do, he wanted to do by himself, without Bob's influence. Smith was his property, his concern. "I'll meet you on the corner of Thirty-fourth Street and Fifth Avenue. Okay?"

"Okay," Bob said, doubtfully.

"Don't worry," Fred reassured him. "I'm not going to kill the boy." Then he laughed at the absurdity of the idea.

So did Bob—unhappily. He also said unhappily, "I didn't think you would. Anyway, I'll see you tomorrow morning."

"Yeah. Thirty-fourth and Fifth."

"Fine."

Fred hung up and turned back to the fallen Smith. He went over to him and took the scarf off him and the sock out of his mouth. The boy had stopped crying, but his blotched, miserable face was looking evil and spiteful.

"Coward," he said.

Fred smiled at him—quite easily—and felt, for the first time, that he was really in command of the situation. "Yeah," he said affably. "Maybe I am. But I was playing your game before, and it wouldn't have worked. Now we're going to play mine."

"Will you *please* untie my hands." Smith tried petulance now.

"No."

"I have to pee."

"Pee in your pants."

"I'll ruin your carpet."

"And I'll make you clean it," Fred said pleasantly.

"You've spoiled *everything*. I should never have come here. First you have that other guy who shares this place with you, and then you let him tell you what to do. You're weak, just like all the rest."

"You should have done your homework better."

"You can't just keep me here."

"Why not?" Fred said, an idea coming to him. "Who's going to miss you?"

"My grandmother, for one."

"What'll she do?"

"She'll ask the police to look for me if I don't turn up."

"The police aren't going to waste their time looking for a creep like you. And even if they did—they'd never find you here. You're a secret, like this apartment."

"How long," Smith drawled flatly, still lying on the floor but suddenly recovering his social manner, "are you planning to keep me here?"

"I'm not sure," Fred said, the idea that had come to him taking form now and settling comfortably. "But maybe—forever." He smiled again. "I won't let Bob come here any more, as I'm buying him out. No one will ever come here any more. Ever. But you'll be here."

A prisoner. Forever. Oh, yes . . . perhaps it was more than just a good idea. Perhaps it was an idea that would have occurred to him no matter what, sooner or later. Maybe, in a way, he had willed Smith upon himself. He suddenly pictured the weeks, and the months, and the years ahead; the years of work, and the changes of season, and the promotions and the money and the easy, regular life; and more than ever they seemed full of promise and hope and happiness. He would come to his secret world every day, and in his secret world he would have his dream; only in this dream—which was, paradoxically, his reality—there would be, as perhaps there always should have been, someone else. A reminder of the so-called real world; a reminder that the Enemy was outside, and would always be there, ready to destroy him if he ever made a slip. Without such a reminder he might get careless.

But with a hostage, a representative of the Enemy—which was how he had first thought of Smith, and was indeed what Smith was—he would never forget. He would have a slave in his kingdom: a slave to represent the weak and the guilty; to represent all those people who were destroying the land, and who would destroy him if they got the chance. And hadn't he envisaged, in his dream of society, a class of slaves, of voluntary slaves who submitted to the rule of the strong? And what was Smith if not a voluntary slave? He had come to him of his own free will and cast himself into chains; and now he would stay with him. And so his apartment, his secret world, would become a microcosm of the world as it should have been, where the weak—who loved guilt—were the ruled, and where the strong and the innocent—those who didn't know the meaning of guilt—were the rulers.

"Forever," Smith echoed, sounding unsurprised, unafraid, almost uninterested.

"That's what you wanted, isn't it?" Fred murmured deeply.

Smith wrinkled his nose. Then he jiggled his shoulders. "I don't know. Maybe."

"Your wanting me to kill you was a trap. It wouldn't have worked. It was just some sort of kick you were trying to get. Like playing Russian roulette."

Smith smiled. "Well, you *might* have killed me. But I doubt it."

It was the sort of trick the weak always played on the strong—trying to make them guilty. . . .

"I was planning to shoot you as soon as we got outside, more or less."

"First of all, you wouldn't have shot me—ever. You'd have lost your nerve. And second, if you had somehow got your nerves together and pulled the trigger—well, I guessed you'd do it as soon as we got outside. Depending on how strong *my* nerves were, I figured I would either start running as soon as I put a foot outside the door, or make some sort of noise in the basement so you couldn't shoot me there." He smiled again, languidly. "What I was really planning to do, one way or another, was to get completely away from you. That way you'd really have been on the rack. Not knowing where I was, what I was going to do."

Once again Fred felt the boy start to weave a web of madness about him, a web that would trap him if he wasn't careful.

But he said, "And will you try to get away now?"

Smith laughed. "Oh, I can't tell you that, can I? That'd be against the rules. I guess if I get tired I'll just stick my head through a window and call for help. Someone'll hear me eventually. Or I'll make a phone call. Or call down to the doorman. And you can't go away and leave me tied and gagged for too long; otherwise I'll die of thirst. And you wouldn't want that, would you?"

"You can survive eight hours without water."

"I guess," Smith murmured.

Fred looked at the boy curiously, and then, feeling that he might be told the truth at last, he said slowly, "Why *did* you come here?"

But Smith only frowned and sighed. "Jesus. I thought I'd made that clear. I've told you enough. I wanted to confess."

"You've got nothing to confess to. Apart from the fact that you're crazy, and you like to play sick games."

"But you can't be sure. I might just be playing games

now. But that doesn't mean to say that what I've told you about me isn't true." He stared Fred in the eyes. "I *am* the Cop Killer."

"You're not."

"Well you must admit I'm mad enough to be, even if you don't think I am."

Fred said, "Get up."

Smith did so.

"Go back to the bathroom, where you were before."

Smith did so. Fred followed. He untied the boy's hands and told him to strip. When he was naked again, Fred threw his clothes out into the corridor. Then he filled up the basin with water and told him to drink as much as he could. Smith did. Then he moaned. "I'm hungry. I haven't eaten since early this morning."

"I'll bring you some food tomorrow morning. You won't starve."

Smith smiled. "Okay."

Fred tied his hands in front of him, then went down the corridor to Bob's bathroom, took some surgical tape that Bob always kept in case of accidents, returned, and taped the boy's mouth up. When he had finished, he nodded and said, "I'll see you tomorrow morning."

He could see from his eyes that Smith was smiling at him. He muttered, "You're enjoying this, aren't you?"

Smith shrugged.

Fred said, "Well, just to be sure you are, there's one other thing I have to do before I leave. You know—just so we both remember this is only a game."

He saw, finally, a flicker of fear in the boy's eyes. He smiled. "And that's—this."

And as he said "this," he raised his knee and crashed it into the boy's groin. And then, as he fell writhing to the floor, choking through his taped mouth, Fred kicked him in the back. And then he lifted him and hit him again and

82

again in the face. And then he let him fall to the floor, and kicked him again, all over. And then, without another word, he washed the blood off his hands in the basin, walked out of the bathroom, locked the door behind him, and left the apartment.

Next morning at eight he met Bob. Standing in the bright, cold, early morning sun on the corner of 34th Street and Fifth Avenue, watching the cars splash through the brown slush, he told him, "I might have done something mad. But I don't think so. You see, I'm sure that kid isn't the Cop Killer. I *know* he isn't. He's just got some sort of masochistic hang-up, and thought he'd corner us—or me, because he didn't know anything about you—by showing up like that. I think he wanted me to try to kill him or something. But anyway—I let him go. I know it's a risk, but I'm a pretty good judge of character, and I don't think he'll say anything about the apartment to anyone. He's got no reason to. My bet is he'll search around for someone else who's got a blackmailable secret and then, instead of blackmailing them, force them to—deal with him, if you see what I mean. He's crazy, of course, and he'll get himself killed one of these days. But that's his affair. The only thing is—I thought, just in case he does say anything to anyone, out of spite or something, we shouldn't go to the apartment for a while. I'd say a month. Just in case there's someone watching it. And especially you. Because he knows my name, and so I guess if he wants he can do something about me. But—you didn't tell him your name, did you?"

"No," Bob said. "Well, I told him it was Bob, but nothing else."

"So you're safe. I'm pretty sure we both are. But you know—just in case he hangs around and tries to follow you. I think if we both keep away for a month—if at the end of that time nothing's happened, we're okay."

"Yes," Bob said slowly. Was he not quite convinced? Fred tried to think of something else to tell him, to keep him away. But before he could, Bob went on. "I guess we just have to learn to live with threats from people like him if we—you know. That boy was like the manifestation of our guilty conscience, coming to remind us."

Fred tried—successfully, though only barely—to resist the temptation of saying something sarcastic. Guilty conscience, my ass, he told himself. To Bob he merely said, "Well, you're out of it now. In fact, you really don't need to go there ever again, if you don't want. Tomorrow or the day after, I'll call my lawyer and then you won't need to have a guilty conscience any more."

How sincere he sounded. . . .

Bob smiled sadly. "I think I'll always have it. But at least that boy turning up really made me think about myself. Something like that makes you face up to things, and admit things to yourself. You know."

"Yes," Fred agreed, watching a woman in a long gray coat and brown boots step carefully into the middle of a puddle, "I know." He paused. "You didn't take the things you came to collect last night, did you?"

"No. I didn't. But there's no hurry. You can either bring them to me one day, or I'll pick them up myself in a month or so."

"I really think it's better."

"Yes," Bob said, looking gravely at Fred, "you're right."

Did he suspect anything? Fred wondered again, as he went to a hardware store to buy a hammer, some nails and some sealing strips and boards. He would partially sound-proof the bathroom by sealing the window, and he would be less afraid of Smith's making any noise that might be heard. Fred was sure Bob wouldn't go near the apartment again for a month. Or rather, he was sure he wouldn't go near the apartment again ever in his life. Not only had he no reason, but, more than anything, he wouldn't want to know. . . .

Three days later they went together to Fred's lawyer in New Jersey—a discreet man who was also the lawyer of some of Fred's financiers, and who didn't know, or didn't care to know, that his clients were policemen—and signed the papers relating to Bob's sale of his half-share in the apartment. Fred gave Bob a check, and Bob, as he took it, shook Fred's hand. And then they made their separate ways back to Manhattan.

The weather, after the snow, became fine and stayed fine, and for three whole weeks the air was crisp and bright and clear. As he went about his work, as he followed his daily routine of buying the *Times,* and as he went to the apartment, Fred felt that he had never before been so sure of himself, so happy, or so certain of man's mastery over the world. The whole enormous granite-based city of New York had never been so vibrant and yet so settled; never had the ordered, symbolic streets and buildings been so challenging, so defiant of the shifting earth. They were here, they seemed to proclaim to the blue winter skies; let tremors, winds, or merely the first, tentative buds menace them—they would rise again brighter, taller, stronger. They might be attacked—by invaders from without or barbarians from within—but they would always, in one form or other, survive. They would *always* survive, because they were not just steel and concrete. They were ideals.

Man would win, they seemed to say. Man had to win.

Oh, how happy he was. . . .

And the reason for his happiness, for his exhilaration and sense of power, was, he knew, Smith. The existence and the presence of the mean, weak boy, battered and beaten, a groveling prisoner in the apartment, honed him and polished him and ground him to a point, as if he were the sharpest, deadliest knife that had ever been wielded in the world.

He had only had to beat him up savagely once more, before the boy abandoned his presumption of playing a game, the rules of which he had invented, and became the frightened, wretched animal that he really was. For now, he simply stayed in the bathroom, whimpering or sleeping or, possibly, thinking; lying on the floor most of the time, with handcuffs on his wrists (the ties with which Fred had bound him, his fine silk ties, he had had to throw away), a rope around his ankles, and surgical tape bound tightly around his face from his scalp—which Fred had shaved—to his chin, so that he could sip water through a straw but couldn't open his jaw enough to shout or make any sound other than a sort of croak.

Once a day Fred would come and remove the tape—which always made the boy wince; it hurt him—and give him his daily meal, which was served in an enormous dog bowl on the floor, and which always consisted of an abundant mixture of rice, chopped-up meat, greens, raw eggs, yogurt, pieces of cheese and fruit. When Smith, on his hands and knees like a dog, his hands still chained together, had gobbled this (in Fred's opinion) sufficient and well-balanced meal, he would finally, and briefly, have the handcuffs removed so that he could shit and wipe himself (there had been some problems about this for the first few days, but after that the boy's bowel movements had become as regular as Fred's visits), take a shower, wash himself, dry himself, and then shave his chin, cheeks and scalp with an electric shaver. Fred never left him for an instant throughout these operations—though he did turn his head away when the boy was sitting on the toilet—and he was always prepared for Smith to make the slightest move, or even to speak, which Fred had forbidden him to do. At the smallest provocation, Fred would leap on him and beat him up again.

The only luxury he allowed the boy was a radio, which he could turn on and off with his chained hands, though Fred had removed the button which controlled the volume so he couldn't turn it up too loud and possibly attract attention.

And just as Fred wished that the bright crisp weather and his crisp bright mood would last forever, so he never allowed himself to think that anything might alter the situation in the apartment. In fact, after only ten days, he couldn't imagine the apartment without Smith. He envisaged the years passing, and his retirement, and Smith in the boarded-up bathroom, getting older and fatter and steadily more docile, like an old dog who has forgotten that he was ever allowed out to run in the park; and Fred was so comforted by the idea that he would have wished the years could pass as quickly as days, if he weren't enjoying the days so much. Of course, he imagined what might happen if he had an accident, or couldn't get to the apartment for some other reason, but he figured that he would never be away for more than a few days, so even if Smith got very hungry, he wouldn't actually die, since there was always a big bowl of water and a lot of straws on the floor alongside the dog's bowl, and he could always drink. If he had a fatal accident—well, yes, the boy would die. That would be too bad, Fred thought, but there was no point in worrying about such things; he had never had an accident in his life, nor, as far as he could remember, had he ever been sick. If anything unexpected did happen, he would just have to deal with it as best he could.

But after three weeks the weather—as it had to—broke; and that same day several things happened.

It was a Tuesday morning, in the second week of March, and Fred arrived at his usual time, with his shoes wet and his hands cold. He went into the kitchen to prepare Smith's meal, and when he had done so he took it in its plastic bowl down the corridor to the bathroom. It was when he unlocked the door that he noticed something odd. Normally when Smith heard him coming he stood up—as he had been instructed—and turned the lights on if they weren't on already. But today the room, with its sealed windows, was dark. As soon as Fred saw this, he backed out into the corridor and set the dog bowl down on the floor; he was ready and on guard in case, in some way, Smith had gotten free and was going to attack him.

But there was no movement within the bathroom, and no sound either. Carefully, Fred slipped a hand around the doorjamb and hit the light switch.

His first thought was that he need not have feared an attack, for Smith was sitting on the floor, with his back against the wall opposite the door. His second thought was that the boy was looking very strange—his face and his lips were terribly white; and if it hadn't been for the redness around his eyes and the wet, shifty blueness of the eyes themselves, Fred would have thought he was dead. He went over to him, checked that his hands were still secure, and then started to rip the tape from the boy's head. Smith didn't make a sound.

Like a short-tempered old nurse, Fred demanded, "What's wrong with you?"

Smith gazed at him; and then, only just moving his white lips, he whispered, "Can I speak?"

"Yes."

"I can't stand any more," the boy said.

Fred, the nurse used to complaining patients, gave a quick, contemptuous laugh. "You've only been here ten days. You wait till you've been here ten years and then tell me how you feel."

Slowly, Smith shook his head. He said, "They'll find me. They'll come looking for me soon."

Fred sighed, went out into the corridor, picked up the dog bowl, and put it on the floor near the boy.

"Here," he muttered, "eat your food. No one's going to come looking for you. I told you before. The police aren't going to bother about a creep like you."

Smith closed his eyes and seemed to hesitate before speaking again. Then he opened them again, and said softly, "Yes they will. My grandmother's very rich."

"All the money in the world isn't going to find you here."

Smith moved his head slightly. "Yes it is. You see—if they look for me, they'll find me. I left a notebook saying where I was. Saying where I was going."

He was bluffing. He had to be bluffing. "You *what?*" Fred whispered, clenching his fists, ready to hit the boy.

Smith closed his eyes again, preparing for the blow. When it didn't come, he said, "I'm not bluffing. I swear. I kept a notebook—a sort of diary—telling the whole story. Except for the ending. I didn't know what the ending would be."

"And where is this notebook?"

"In a desk in my room in my grandmother's house in Providence."

Fred bit his lips; he had to think clearly. "And you've written my name and address in your book?"

Almost imperceptibly, Smith nodded.

"And so if someone starts to look for you, they'll find it?"

There was a long pause before the boy spoke again, and when he did, he whispered flatly, "They *are* looking for me. I heard it on the news on the radio this morning. There was just a little thing about me."

Fred felt the blood leaving his face; he thought he would fall over. He closed the seat of the toilet and sat on it. But then, as he sat there, something struck him.

"If that's true, why are you telling me? Why don't you just wait for someone to show up here?"

Smith swallowed, his Adam's apple jerking in his thin, flaky white neck. "Because I want to give you a chance. Maybe they haven't found the notebook yet. If you let me go, I'll go to the police and tell them I heard the thing on the news, and that I'm alive and well, and then they'll stop looking for me. And you'll be safe. I won't tell anyone."

Fred didn't believe him. "Why do you want to give me a chance?"

"Because it's not really your fault that I'm here, is it? I mean—I came willingly." He sighed. "I swear I won't tell them about you."

Still sitting on the toilet, Fred closed his eyes for a second. Then he repeated, "Why are you telling me this? Why don't you just wait for them to find you here and arrest me?"

Smith whispered, sounding totally defeated now, "I was going to. But then—well, I've been thinking these last few days—it's just possible that they won't find the notebook. They might. But they might not. Or they might not for months, anyway. And I can't stand this any more. I can't go on. So I thought—in case they do find it—I'd give you a chance. And in return—you let me go."

"And if I don't?"

"Sooner or later they will find it."

"And if they already have?"

"If I go to the police right away, then they wouldn't do

anything probably. About you." Smith paused. There was, Fred felt, a note of falsity in his voice now; something slightly theatrical. "They'll arrest me, I guess. Because I've written about all the killings. But not about you. I mean—you could take me in. They'd be so pleased with you for having arrested me that they wouldn't do anything about this place. I mean—they don't really care about corrupt cops, do they? And they'd have to prove that the money you bought this place with and maintain it with comes from—" He shrugged. "You could say it was your father's or something. You could say anything. They won't care. Not if you've arrested the Cop Killer."

Fred stared at the boy. "You're not the Cop Killer."

Smith shrugged again; and now when he spoke there was no longer any hint of the theatrical in his voice. He sounded simply very tired. "I *say* I am," he whispered.

Fred continued to bite his lips. "How well-hidden is the notebook?"

"It's behind a drawer in my desk. Only the drawer is sort of difficult to get out. And I guess unless they were actually looking for it—no one does."

"Your grandmother?"

"No."

"Do you have any maids, servants, anyone?"

"My grandmother has a couple of women who come in every day to cook and clean for her. But they don't poke around in my room. I'm sure they haven't found it yet."

"And if I let you go now—?"

"Then I'll go back to Providence and destroy the notebook and everything will be over." He paused. "And there'll be no more killings. Because you know, and I know—" He shrugged once more. And then, suddenly, his face crumpled like a piece of soiled paper crushed in someone's hand, and he burst into tears. "Please let me go," he sobbed. "Please. I can't stand any more."

"And if this story about the notebook is all a lie?"

"It isn't," the boy cried. "I swear it isn't. Just let me go. Please."

Fred watched him as he kneeled in front of him; watched him without saying a word for some time. And then he said, "Eat your food."

"No," Smith whimpered. "I can't. It's disgusting. I can't eat any more of that stuff. Oh, *please* let me go."

Fred didn't insist; again, he simply watched the boy, as a plan formed in his head. "What's your grandmother's name?" he said quietly.

"Archell-Smith. Marguerite Archell-Smith."

"And her address?"

"Why?"

"What's her address?"

The red-rimmed eyes grew larger. Smith whispered again, "Why?"

"Because," Fred said, getting up and going over to the shelf to fetch the surgical tape, "I'm going up to Providence to see your grandmother. And to see if your notebook exists. If it does, and it's still there, I'll destroy it. And if it doesn't, and your grandmother tells me that the police haven't found anything, I'll come back and beat you into a pulp. And if your grandmother says it has been found—" he smiled, pleasantly—"I hope I'll get back here before anyone else does, so I can kill you. If I'm going to lose all this, you can be damn sure that you're going to pay for it. And they can send me to prison for life if they like. Because—" and he smiled again at the boy, though slightly madly this time—"all this is my freedom. And if they take this away from me, I'll be in prison anyway."

Smith—as Fred advanced toward him, holding the surgical tape in his hands—got to his feet and backed against the wall. He was shaking his head wildly from side to side. "You can't," he whispered. "You can't. I was giving you a chance. You can't do this."

Fred shrugged. "Who says I can't?"

Smith's head went on shaking. "No," he gasped. "Please. I can't stand it any more. Please. Don't do it."

Fred pulled off a length of tape.

"No," Smith gasped again. "No. No—"

But before he could scream, Fred put his big red hand over the boy's mouth, and, ignoring the teeth that were biting into him, started slowly to bind the shaven head.

When he had finished, and Smith had fallen to the ground, weeping, he said, "I'll come around as soon as I get back. And try not to shit in the meantime. You can wash and shave and have your meal then. Unless," he added as he went out the door, "I have to kill you."

He called in sick—making a joke of it: he, sick, who had never been sick in his life!—and then took the subway directly to Grand Central Station. He had to wait an hour for a train to Providence, but he spent that hour reading the paper, which he had bought, without a moment's hesitation, from the newsstand at the station.

The article he wanted to see—a tiny one—was under the headline: "Rhode Island Heir Vanishes."

When, at two o'clock that afternoon, he arrived in Providence, he bought the local paper, which gave the news in greater detail. It also gave the address of Mrs. Marguerite Archell-Smith: the Austrian-born widow of cotton millionaire John Archell-Smith, Jr., whose grandson, Leo, had not been seen or heard from now for more than three weeks.

Then he took a taxi to within a block of the house—which was, as he had imagined, big and white—and waited outside for a while in the gray, blustery March afternoon, to check that there were no patrol cars around. Then, telling himself that if there were any police or reporters inside the house (though after hanging around almost three-quarters of an hour, he doubted it), he would bluff his way out of the situation somehow, he walked up to the big green front door and rang the bell.

CHAPTER 6

An old shapeless woman in an old skirt, shapeless sweater and thick brown stockings, with a face that was smudged and worn like an eraser that had erased too much, opened the door, peered at Fred through glasses whose frames had been repaired with a Band-Aid, and raised her eyebrows. She was carrying a walking stick, and Fred guessed she was an old servant who could probably no longer climb the stairs.

He flashed his badge at her quickly and said, "Lieutenant Franklin, ma'am. I'd like to speak to Mrs. Archell-Smith."

The old woman gave him a slight, twisted smile—as if she were smiling at something private—and asked, "Is there some news about Leo?" She had a slight foreign accent.

"No. I'm afraid not. Not yet. I'd like to ask Mrs. Archell-Smith one or two more questions about Leo's—habits, character."

"She told the other officers everything." She pronounced it "everytink," and said it with an air of finality.

"Yeah, I know," Fred insisted. He began to feel appre-

95

hensive and wondered if this old maid was going to let him into the house at all. She didn't seem about to, and she was still smiling her private smile.

But, after studying Fred for a while, she obviously made up her mind. Very pleasantly, and sounding now very foreign, she said, "Please come in, officer."

Limping, she led him through a high, dark hallway that was hung with two faded tapestries and furnished with several massive carved chests and chairs, and into a large, bright living room that looked, Fred thought, like a furniture depository. There were too many chairs—all worn—of different shapes and sizes; too many sofas of different colors; and too many tables, sideboards and bookcases. And everything there, apart from being worn and looking as if, even long ago when it wasn't worn, it hadn't been very attractive, was arranged without any order or even, apparently, sense. A large green sofa faced a blank wall; four spindle-legged chairs were set in a circle with their backs to one another, facing outward; one large bookcase was inaccessible, being behind a table; and another table—a great dark oak thing that stood in front of some French windows one could clearly get neither in nor out of—was surrounded on the three sides that were not against the windows by two vast brocaded armchairs, two bamboo garden chairs, and two white plastic armchairs, all of which were so low that the only thing one could have done comfortably at the table would have been to rest one's chin on it.

The old woman led Fred through this maze of abandoned furniture as if she were blind and had learned her way around by heart, and sat him down on a high, wooden-backed sofa whose hard seat was covered with some tattered fabric and smelled vaguely of cat urine. Then she said, "Just a moment please."

She threaded her way back out of the room and closed

the door behind her, leaving Fred to study the furniture and to look out through the blocked windows onto a big garden that was as ordered and neat and well laid out as the living room was not. He also had time to wonder if the other maid, who was presumably younger, worked in the afternoon—and time to hope not. It would be easier for him if he could be in Leo's room alone, without some curious servant peering over his shoulder to see what he was doing and thinking it odd that he should pull out the drawers of the vanished boy's desk.

He was alone for about five minutes, and was anxiously watching the closed door through which the old woman had gone, and wishing that her employer would come soon so he could do what he had to do and get out, when he heard another door, behind him, open.

He rose instinctively to his feet and turned to greet Leo Smith's grandmother. The woman he saw advancing across the room to welcome him, however, was not, as he had imagined, some grand old New England dame (New England in spite of her Austrian birth), but the same old lady who had let him in the door, smiling now even more twistedly but as if at last Fred could share in the joke.

"Officer," she said, "how nice to see you. Please sit down. I'm so sorry to have kept you waiting." At first she sounded to Fred like one of those old eternal refugees who people the streets of New York; and then he thought that the old woman had a strange sense of humor. Sure, he had thought she was a servant, and had possibly spoken to her as if he thought she was; but then it was equally possible that he hadn't, and that she simply enjoyed playing her own maid—or confusing her visitors. However, he told himself, there was nothing to be gained by feeling annoyed or by letting the joke antagonize him—so he shook hands with her as if absolutely nothing unusual had occurred. As if he were meeting her for the first time. He said, "I'm sorry to have to disturb you. You must be sick of the police and reporters by now."

Marguerite Archell-Smith raised her old eyebrows and said, "Yes? Must I?" Then she pulled a face, smiled very pleasantly, and murmured gently, "Oh, no. I love to meet new people. Whoever they are. I'm just sorry I have to meet you in here. But I'm having my living room re-painted."

Fred smiled and said, "Ah, I guessed maybe you were."

"I'm not," the old lady said, chuckling. "I was lying to you. This is my living room." She put her hand on Fred's arm and lowered herself onto the sofa beside him. "You must forgive me. I'm a wicked old woman. But I can never resist telling people what they want to hear. And I al-ways—or nearly always—know. But then I get ashamed of myself, because it's really rather a cruel trick to play. Do forgive me."

Fred smiled again, but rather more doubtfully this time. He wasn't certain how to get onto the subject of Leo with this strange old creature.

While he was wondering, however, the old creature got onto the subject herself. "So," she said, sounding serious at last, "there's no more news about Leo."

"No, ma'am," Fred said. He cleared his throat. "But I would like it if you could tell me again about Leo's habits." He cleared his throat once more.

"Everything?"

"Yes, ma'am. You never know, you might have forgotten something the first time. Some little thing that might give us a clue as to where Leo's gotten to."

"I forgot nothing," Marguerite Archell-Smith said, "but I don't mind repeating myself." She wrinkled up her old, smudged nose. "Leo's silly. He's a weak-minded boy who's had a good education, which is always a dangerous thing for people with weak minds. He'll probably end up being

President." She chuckled again at her own wit and scratched one of her thick brown woolen knees. "Or perhaps I should say he's giddy rather than silly. Because at times he's very sweet, and almost bright. Anyway, I like having him about." She said it decisively, as if that settled that. Then she pulled a pack of cigarettes from the sleeve of her sweater, offered one to Fred, took one herself, lit it carefully as if it were likely to explode in her face, and continued, "He's a masochist." She glanced slyly at Fred now, clearly hoping she had knocked him with her bald announcement. She had, too. She said it in such a matter-of-fact way, as if being a masochist were no more unusual or interesting than being a person with two legs. "He likes to have pain inflicted on him. He likes to be mistreated, and beaten, and—well, I think you know what a masochist is, Lieutenant. That's Leo's only habit, and that's why I'm worried that something's happened to him. I'm afraid that he met someone in New York who might have gratified his desires, shall we say, too completely. But I know nothing about his life when he goes to New York, and nothing about his friends, if he has any, which I'm not sure about. I hate to interfere in anyone's life—unless it's unavoidable. I called the police because I thought it was now."

Trying to sound businesslike, though now he felt almost disgusted by the old lady's acceptance of her grandson's perversion, Fred inquired, "Weren't you worried that he might get hurt? I mean, before now?"

"Of course I was. But I'd only have made it worse if I'd disapproved, or pretended to know nothing. I thought that by talking to Leo about it and treating it as if it were something entirely natural—which I suppose it is, even if it's not very pleasant—I'd help him to get over it, make him see how silly he was being. He even showed me some photographs he had. They were horrible. . . . But the thing that made me hope that talking about it openly

99

might help it to pass was that Leo's masochism wasn't just physical. If it had been, I'd have thought that the only thing to do would be to persuade him to go to a psychiatrist, much as I disapprove of psychiatrists. But as it was, Leo had a whole lot of pseudo-philosophical mumbo jumbo with which he tried to justify his sexual tastes, and which might just have been responsible for his starting to put his fantasies into practice."

She puffed smoke out into the air, laid her hand on Fred's arm again, and leaned toward him. "I think it is always difficult to know whether our fears and desires shape our moral choices, Lieutenant, or whether our moral choices shape our fears and desires. I prefer to think the latter, otherwise there is really no hope for the human race. But I'm always afraid it's the former. Anyway—" she sighed now and released Fred's arm—"Leo had this idea that only through pain can we really become conscious of ourselves and the world. He said it was as if he preferred going into hell to face the monsters, rather than continually pretending that the monsters didn't exist, and being at their mercy if and when they did suddenly spring out of the darkness and attack him. He was also convinced that all the money he was going to inherit was damned money, money earned out of other people's suffering, and that he somehow had to atone for all that." She smiled sadly. "I did try to tell him that the monsters in his hell were just imaginary, and that there was no great merit in facing up to something he only imagined, and, what's more, that he wasn't responsible for his grandfather's and great-grandfather's wickedness, though I'm prepared to admit that both my husband and his father were wicked. I told him that one could no more be damned by the sins of one's ancestors than one could be saved by their virtues. But he wouldn't believe me." She turned around to face Fred. "You must meet with a lot of this in your work, Lieutenant. Why *are* people so willing and eager to be guilty?"

"I don't know, ma'am," Fred said softly, not wanting to interrupt the old lady's slow, gentle, accented speech, which he was rather enjoying.

She took a deep drag on her cigarette before she continued. "Anyway, as I said, I failed." She gave a dry little laugh. "The really painful thing for me about it—I mean apart from his disappearance now—is that he was started on all this a few years ago by a series of really dreadful, trite articles in some magazine, by some dreadful, trite woman who wrote about the police and had some half-baked notions that the police were not so much the guardians and preservers of our safety as they were the guardians and preservers of our danger—the manifestations of our desire for chaos, rather than the manifestations of our desire for order." Marguerite Archell-Smith snorted. "It was something like that. I can't remember exactly. But it was all mostly potted Freud—the police satisfying our longing for guilt, and inspiring us to commit crimes just so we can be punished for them. I'm not saying that some of it might not be true in a way, but the basic idea was that the police were all wretches whom we'd be better off without, even if the woman who wrote the articles was much too sharp ever to come out into the open and say such a damn fool thing. What so many of these liberals would like is some mixture of self-condemnation and self-punishment, and college-educated lynching parties." She gave an old Austrian laugh. "I'm a liberal myself. Did you ever see those articles, Lieutenant?"

"No," Fred said, not wanting to seem surprised by this coincidence (he wasn't; it seemed entirely natural to him, and quite inevitable), nor wanting to tell Leo Smith's grandmother that he not only had read them, and knew the girl who had written them, but that he himself had been intended as material for those articles.

"Do you remember the woman's name? The one who wrote the articles?"

"No. Besides, Leo wrote her a couple of letters asking her about some points she had made, but he never got a reply. So she wouldn't know anything about him. But it was really with those articles that the trouble began. Leo got this obsession with the police and was always threatening to go and confess to any crimes he read about in the paper. Once, about two years ago, he actually did. A girl was raped and murdered here, and Leo rushed off and told the police that he had done it. Luckily the captain knew me, and phoned me, and I went and sorted it all out."

Fred asked slowly, "Did Leo do it?"

Marguerite Archell-Smith gave another old laugh. "You're smart, Mr.—?"

"Franklin."

"Mr. Franklin. No. Leo didn't do it. But I'm afraid that one day he might confess to something that his old grandmother with her cursed millions won't be around to help him out of."

"You don't think he's confessed to something and is being held somewhere now—under another name?"

As soon as he had said it, he realized it was a mistake; and the old lady realized it, too. She said, "I was hoping you would be able to tell me that, Mr. Franklin. Your colleagues said yesterday that his photograph was being sent around the country."

"Yes," Fred mumbled, trying to get out of it, "but I wondered whether *you* thought that's what's happened?"

"I don't know. But it is possible. That's one of the reasons I asked for your help." She sounded, now, slightly annoyed.

"Yes, of course." Fred cleared his throat and changed the subject. "You said that Leo had some photographs. You don't know if he still has them, do you? It might be useful if we could identify some of the people in those photographs—if they're not only of Leo."

"No. They were not only of Leo," the old lady retorted. "But I also told your colleagues yesterday that I haven't seen them for years, and Leo told me that he had destroyed them."

Was she beginning to get suspicious? Fred wondered. He tried, with a laugh, to smooth things over. "I guess you think we're not very well coordinated."

"No. I wasn't thinking that at all. I am truly grateful for any help you can give me, and if to help you help me I have to repeat myself—I told you, I don't mind."

She sounded sincere, Fred thought. He came at last to the point. "Well, do you think you could help me more by letting me take a look at Leo's room?"

"Yes, of course," the old lady said, starting to rise slowly. "I did look myself, of course, but it is possible I overlooked something. I was," she added, "quite surprised your colleagues yesterday didn't want to poke around."

It was as easy as that.

The notebook, as Leo Smith had said, was behind the drawer in his desk. Fred opened the first page, read the words, "I am the Cop Killer," and put the book in his pocket. Then he sat on a red-silk-covered bed for ten minutes, looking around the characterless, paintingless room—furnished only with the bed, the desk, a brown rug and a wooden chair—before going downstairs to tell the boy's grandmother that he had found nothing.

As Fred was leaving the house he said, "Do you mind if I ask you a personal question, Mrs. Smith?"

"Oh, you can ask me anything, Mr. Franklin," the old lady muttered—sarcastically?

"Why," Fred said, "did a nice lady like you marry a man who you knew was wicked?"

Marguerite Archell-Smith laughed. "You *are* smart, Mr. Franklin. But the truth of the matter is, I didn't know that my husband was wicked when I married him. He was quite a bit older than I, and belonged to a different world. And just when I did find out, he was killed in an accident." She gave Fred a last, twisted, private smile. "I was lucky," she said, "wasn't I?"

On the train back to New York he read Leo's notebook. It was in three parts. The first consisted of a detailed account of how the boy had killed the six policemen—complete with time, place, method of selection and pursuit, mode of attack, and death agonies. The last one was rather sketchy, and had obviously been written up in a hurry. There were also photographs, cut from the papers, and notes on the murdered men's families.

The second part of the notebook consisted of a number of very short pornographic stories, fantasies really. All of them (though Fred didn't read them, but merely glanced disgustedly through them) were of the most repulsive nature. They were told in the first person, and consisted mainly of how the narrator, Leo Smith, was beaten, humiliated, tortured, and frequently murdered. At the end of the last story, after the narrator had described how—and with what sensations—he had had his fingernails ripped from his hands, his eyes gouged out, his genitals sawn off, and, finally, been impaled on a red-hot iron spike, there was written, by way of a postscript:

This is my theater and my reality; this is my art and my life. I have been to the center of the earth, and flown to the edge of space—into the total darkness where the hardest diamond melts like snow on a summer's day, and into the regions where time curves. I have been where no one else has ever been, and I have borne what no one else has ever borne. I have been the Sahara, rained on by the dark clouds of knowledge, and I have absorbed every drop; I have been the ice caps of the poles, dissolved by the warm currents of consciousness. I have been everything, I have done everything, I have known everything. I have lived.

The third part of the notebook was, for Fred, the most interesting. It read:

February 29. I have found him. I am absolutely certain. And he is exactly as I hoped he would be. A great red sow of a man. A sow, yes, not a pig; there is something gentle, almost maternal, about the way he walks and moves, in spite of his size, and in spite of the fact that there is nothing soft about him. It is as if there were small invisible piglets surrounding him and he was scared of treading on them, or small invisible piglets feeding on him and he was scared of disturbing them. I knew as soon as I saw him that he was my man. I followed him for a while and then I lost him. It was almost as if he knew he was being followed, and was trying to lose me—which is very unlikely. But the fact that I did lose him only makes me more sure of my choice. Tomorrow, or the day after, I will find him again.

March 2. I have, as I knew I would, found him again. And once again he tried to lose me. But this time I was more careful. I followed him all over town. He went up to W. 104th St. to buy a newspaper, and then went—by way of Second Avenue and E. 23 St.!—to an apartment house on Central Park West. #88.

March 10. His name is Frank O'Connor.

March 11. He is called Fred, and is a lieutenant.

March 18. He lives in a run-down brownstone on Prospect Park West. (Central Park West—Prospect Park West—any connection?)

March 26. I have followed him every day for the last six days. Everything about him is beyond my wildest dreams.

April 8. Five days up here in Providence. I wonder how Fred is doing. I can't wait to get back to N.Y. to see.

April 9. I would like to introduce Fred to Grandmother. I'm sure she'd love him!

June 12. I feel I'm ready, but I must be patient. There must be no mistakes. I think perhaps this winter sometime. I would prefer it if I could get a look at the apartment on C.P.W. one day when he's out—but it's too risky.

June 26. How much can one know about another human being just by watching, following, listening? Everything, I think—far more, anyway, than by talking to someone, which tends to confuse one. We put up so many smoke screens. But I won't be certain until—

July 19. Fred is on vacation. Bless him. I knew he wouldn't go away.

September 22. He looked right at me today. I was afraid he'd seen me. But he was looking through me. Searching for the dark horseman, I guess. Or checking on his invisible piglets. Certainly he would never suspect *me*.

September 23. He looked through me again today. Is it possible, I wonder, that subconsciously he *does* know I am following him, and is happy about it? Which is why he never sees me when he looks at me. The idea is quite exciting. If it's true, I guess we could keep this up forever. Or until I get bored. And then I'll make him see me.

December 1. Quite soon now. Next week I'd better fix a date, otherwise I might keep putting it off and putting it off. (Which makes me suspect that just as Fred must subconsciously know I'm following him, so I, subconsciously, might be afraid of him, and of going through with my plan. If so—no! If so, nothing. Fuck my subconscious.)

December 29. I *am* afraid.

January 20. I must let him see me. That way, whether I like it or not, the ball will start rolling.

February 8. Tomorrow I shall either let him see me, or I'll go round to the apartment when he's there and have the doorman call up. In case—I'm not sure what in case—but anyway; maybe from tomorrow my address, or my last known address, will be c/o Fred O'Connor, 88 Central Park West, N.Y.C.

When Fred had finished reading he put the notebook back in his pocket. When he got back to the apartment he would burn it, he decided. Or maybe he would tear it up into small pieces, mix it with Smith's food, and make him eat it. . . .

It was a cold, blustery, wild night—around eleven by the time Fred hurried from the subway and walked quickly toward his block; and as he did, he thought how pleasant it would be up in the apartment, with Smith finally beyond help, and himself totally out of danger. How very pleasant, sitting listening to the wind and knowing that he was completely in control. As long as Marguerite Archell-Smith hadn't suspected him, which he didn't think she had, and didn't mention him to anyone, which he didn't think she would, he was completely in control now. Perhaps, he thought, he would call in sick tomorrow too; just so he could enjoy his victory to the full. The lord in his kingdom, with his guilty slave. . . .

Smith was still lying on the floor of the bathroom. He looked at Fred, and at the notebook in his hand, and then closed his eyes.

Fred smiled and said, "I liked your grandmother."

Smith's eyes stayed closed.

Fred put the notebook down on the edge of the bath, went over to the boy, and removed the tape from his head.

"You hungry?" he said

"No," Smith muttered.

"I liked your grandmother," Fred repeated.

"Why?"

Fred was about to answer when he realized that he didn't know. After all, the old lady, with her disturbing living room and odd sense of humor—symptoms of a madness that would develop more fully in the grandchild?—

shouldn't have been the sort of person he liked. And yet he had.

"I'm not sure," he said finally. "But I guess—there's something—regular about her. Straight. She's not weak."

Smith didn't reply. He didn't seem interested in the subject of his grandmother, or in anything else. He simply lay there, with his shaven head and red-rimmed eyes, and gazed at the notebook as if it were a dream he had had and now had lost forever, or as if he were consciously, purposely avoiding Fred's eyes.

"What happened to your parents?"

Now the boy did look up at him and, strangely, gave him a sort of smile. "My father died of drink at the age of thirty-six. He was my grandmother's son. My mother got married again three months after his death, and killed herself on the second day of her honeymoon. She thought she had married someone rich and discovered that her new husband only had a rich mother who gave him pocket money when he begged for it. Like my father. I reckon she couldn't stand having made the same mistake twice. Or perhaps there were other reasons." The smile, even more strangely, became almost intimate. "They were weak, both of them, and my grandmother destroyed them." Then the smile faded, and once again the boy became expressionless; expressionless as one who has been defeated and knows it, or—Fred stared at him suddenly, struck by something about the pose of the thin white body—expressionless as one who is trying hard to conceal some expression, some emotion. Because he *wasn't* completely defeated-looking, as he should have been. There was a tension about him, an air of expectancy, that there shouldn't have been under the circumstances. After all, everything that was ever going to happen to him in his whole life *had* happened. But—Fred shook his head. He was imagining things.

"I think your grandmother liked me," he said.

"She likes everyone," Smith muttered. "'Specially if they're mad."

Fred wondered whether he should hit him. He decided not to. There was no point in it any longer. He had won, and Smith, however he behaved, whatever he said, had lost.

"Do you want to shit?"

"No. Not now."

Why not? Fred wondered. What *was* he waiting for? "I read your notebook," he said. "Or should I say, your novel."

Smith nodded but didn't reply.

"You better eat your food anyway. Even if you're not hungry."

"Okay."

Smith crawled over to the dog bowl and knelt in front of it. And then, just as he seemed about to start lapping up the mush, he suddenly looked up at Fred again. Only this time he looked up, not with a smile, but with a look of unmistakable contempt, scorn and, somehow, triumph. The transformation shocked Fred and made him nervous. He demanded, "What the hell are you looking at me like that for?"

The boy's lips opened and closed; and now he seemed about to laugh. He went on staring at Fred—at him, but also through him, and past him—and then whispered, "You thought you'd won, didn't you?"

"What the hell—" Fred started again, taking a step forward. And then he stopped, and froze. He became aware of the sound of the wind and, faintly, in the distance, the sound of cars. He became aware of the bathroom as if he had never seen it before, taking in every detail, every tap and tile. He became aware—horribly aware—of every inch of Smith's wretched body. He could almost count the pale hairs on the thin, flaky arms. And he became aware of the fact that there was someone standing behind him, in the bathroom door.

He turned, slowly.

Bob was pointing a gun at him. He said tragically, "Take the cuffs off the boy, Fred."

Fred obeyed. It wasn't safe to argue with someone who was playing a part he wasn't sure of, and Bob wasn't at all sure of his. Fred also, without being told, untied the boy's feet.

"Get out of here," Bob said to Smith. "Go get some clothes on."

"You can't let him go, Bob," Fred said calmly. "He's the Cop Killer. I've got proof. It's all written down in there." He pointed at the notebook.

Bob glanced at it and muttered, "Good. Then I'm taking him in."

"You can't do that, Bob," Fred said calmly.

"I'm going to," Bob said.

"You realize—"

"Yeah, I realize." Bob stared at Fred, and then looked at the dog bowl on the floor. He said, "You're crazy, Fred."

He said it in his special grim voice—and then suddenly he gave up the unaccustomed part, and rushed on, frowning now, and in his usual *concerned* voice, "You can't do this sort of thing, Fred. Lenore read about the boy's disappearance in the paper and remembered his name, because apparently he wrote her a letter once which she's always kept framed in her office because she thought it was so funny. And when she told me about it, I figured out who it was and guessed that you were still keeping him here. I should have realized before. God, I feel terrible. I'm going to take the boy in and—I'll tell the whole story. I—" Bob's handsome face started to crack with emotion, and with the consciousness of his own nobility. "You're crazy, Fred," he said again, only this time he said it with wonder, and sadness. "How could you have done something like this?"

"I had to have proof."

"But to treat the boy like a dog. To shave his head. To—treat him like this."

"It was the only way to get proof."

"But what were you going to do with this proof?"

"I would have taken him in."

Bob gazed at him, and then, tragically, shook his head. "You wouldn't have, Fred. You know that. You would have kept the boy here, or killed him."

Smith, who had been standing, watching the scene, finally spoke. Sounding once more like a bored, silly society boy playing a game, he announced, "He wouldn't have killed me."

"Go and get dressed," Bob said.

Smith walked out of the bathroom, squeezing past Bob, and called plaintively to Fred, "Where are my clothes?"

"In the closet where they were before," Fred called back. Then, to Bob, he said, "I'll tell you what I was going to do, Bob. As soon as I could, I was going to sell the apartment. I could have moved out in a day. And then I would have taken the boy in. If he'd told some story about me having an apartment on Central Park West—well, everyone'd have said he was crazy."

"There are documents. The doormen could have testified."

"I would have paid the doormen off. And anyway, if I'd brought in the Cop Killer, I don't think anybody would have been about to check up on me seriously. Not even if they'd suspected something. Maybe they'd have called the superintendent here and just asked casually if I had an apartment in the building. And, like I said, if I'd given him a thousand dollars or something, he would have said no, and—no. It would all have been okay, Bob. But I had to be sure he *was* the Cop Killer. Otherwise, if I'd just taken some nut in, I'd have had nothing to bargain with, if you get me."

Bob nodded slowly, unwillingly and unbelievingly. "Why didn't you *tell* me?" he murmured. "I mean, I've seen you every day practically, and all you ever did was just wink and give me the thumbs-up and—all the time you had him here."

"I couldn't have told you," Fred said. He risked a smile. "I knew you were too decent. You'd never have allowed me to do this."

Bob nodded again. "How did you get that notebook?"

"He told me he kept a record of all the murders. It was in his grandmother's house up in Providence. I've been up there today to fetch it. I only got back five minutes ago—as you know," he added bitterly. "How long have you been here?"

"About an hour."

"Why didn't you untie Smith yourself?"

"I would have, but he told me not to. He said I should wait until you were in here talking to him before I showed myself. He said you might come in armed or something. And also—I don't know—I just wanted to see you with him. Just to have proof myself, I guess. I mean—it's all like some sick dream. I couldn't believe you were actually doing this."

The two men looked at each other, both slightly embarrassed, and both uncertain quite what to say now. Finally Fred tried, "Don't you think you should be pointing that gun at Smith rather than me? If you let him get away now—"

Bob gazed at him once more, gazed at him with the eyes of one who had been betrayed, who will be betrayed again, and who can do nothing about it except grieve. And then, slowly, he turned and pointed his gun—but limply now, uncertainly—down the corridor.

Fred didn't hesitate for a second. He jumped. He caught Bob in the back and sent him crashing against the wall.

And then, as they fell together to the floor, he twisted him over and smashed him, as hard as he could, with his fist, in the face. And then he hit him with the side of his hand on the neck. He hit him five times. And then, when Bob lay still at last, he grabbed the gun that had fallen to the floor and, breathing heavily, got slowly to his feet.

Smith, half-dressed but already with his woolen cap on, was staring at Bob on the floor. He looked so shocked—his eyes wide, his mouth open—that Fred wanted to laugh. Then he looked up at Fred and started to back away from him, down the corridor.

"Stay still," Fred said, sounding, he heard, more irritated than commanding.

Smith stopped, and whispered in his flat voice, "Have you killed him?"

Fred—as calm and clear-headed as if he had planned the whole episode in advance—smiled and replied, "No, of course not." And then, as Smith still stared at him, he added pleasantly and reasonably—after all, it was the most obvious thing in the world—"And I'm not going to. You see, Mr. Smith, *you* are."

CHAPTER 7

Fred leaned against the wall of the corridor and smiled at the boy again. He said, "Why not? You're the Cop Killer, aren't you?"

Smith didn't reply. His watery blue eyes looked down at Bob, up at Fred, and down at Bob again. And then, finally, slowly, he shook his head. "No," he whispered.

"No what?"

"I—I can't kill him," Smith stuttered.

"Why not? One more, one less. What's the difference?"

"No."

"Yes."

"No. No. No. No." Smith backed farther down the corridor, toward the living room, whispering "No" as he went. It was only when he was right at the end of the corridor that he whispered, "How?"

Fred closed his eyes for a moment. He felt very tired suddenly. But then he told himself to wake up and to think. He looked down at Bob—Bob in blue jeans and a rust-colored sweater and a heavy blue jacket—and then he started to talk. But he talked quietly, and to himself.

"We'll take him downstairs to the service entrance.

Then—or rather before that—I'll go out and steal a car and park it outside. We'll put him in the car and drive him—" he paused, and then gave a slight smile—"to the park behind the natural history museum. Then we'll make sure no one's about, and we'll take him out of the car and take him into the park, and then—you'll cut his throat with a bread knife." What Fred didn't say was that as soon as Smith had cut Bob's throat he would shoot him—with Bob's gun. And then they would be found together, the Cop Killer and his last victim. He would probably come back to the apartment. It might be difficult to explain how Bob could have shot the boy when he was already—even before his throat was cut—dead, killed by a series of blows to the side of the neck. And he *was* dead, Fred was sure, but he didn't want Smith to know it. The boy had to think that *he* had killed Bob. He had to take this guilt too upon himself.

He ordered, "Go back to the bathroom."

Smith cowered at the end of the corridor and didn't seem about to move. But when Fred lowered his voice and repeated, "Go back to the bathroom," the boy appeared to shudder slightly and then walked slowly toward him, never taking his eyes off Bob. He stepped into the bathroom as if he were in a trance.

Fred followed him, put the handcuffs on him, and tied his feet. Then he sealed his mouth with tape; he couldn't be bothered to bind up the whole head.

"I'll be back," he said, "in five minutes. I hope."

He locked the bathroom door, then walked down the corridor to the hallway and let himself out. He took the elevator down—it was an old brown elevator with paneled wooden walls, and he stroked the wood absentmindedly, as if assuring it too that he would soon be back—and walked out the main door, nodding, with a smile, to the doorman.

He didn't have to steal a car. The service entrance to the building was a green iron door at the bottom of a small flight of steps on West 69th Street. Parked right outside it was a big, light-blue, very suitable-looking Ford station wagon, which Fred had no difficulty in prying open.

He walked around the block a couple of times, and then went back into his building, nodding and smiling once again at the doorman.

He untied Smith's feet and put his scarf over his taped-up mouth. He put on a pair of gloves—fine gloves, which he kept in the closet along with his silk suits and shirts. He went into the kitchen, took the bread knife, and put it into his pocket. (It was a small bread knife, and a large pocket.) He picked up Bob's gun—a snub-nosed .38 pistol —from the floor where he had put it after locking Smith in the bathroom, before he went out to get the car. He put the gun in his pocket, too. Then, with only a little difficulty —he had never felt stronger in his life—he picked Bob up and managed to sling his body over one shoulder. When he had found his balance, he took the gun out of his pocket again, pointed it at Smith, and whispered, "Come on."

They walked, Smith leading, to the back door. Then they stood still for a moment and glanced at each other, as if they both knew that this would be the last time they would see each other in this apartment. Then Fred opened the door and whispered to Smith, "Call the elevator."

He himself stood just inside the door, with Bob hanging off him like a giant fox around an old woman's shoulders, until the elevator arrived.

He whispered to Smith, "Open the door."

The door of the service elevator didn't open automatically. It was an iron grill that made quite a lot of noise as Smith opened it.

Fred, with his human fox-fur, closed the apartment door behind him, stepped into the elevator, closed the iron grill himself, and pressed the button for the basement.

How quiet the building was at night, with only the rattling elevator breaking the silence. . . .

When they stopped, Fred stood still for a moment, the gun in his right hand, pressed into Smith's back. Would there be someone in the basement? he wondered. Would the doorman in the lobby have heard the elevator and come down to investigate? Would Smith try to kick something or make some other noise? He looked at the small amount of face visible between the boy's black cap and the scarf, and frowned at it, menacingly. But Smith didn't seem to see him. He was too scared, Fred guessed.

He whispered very softly, "Open the door, quietly."

Knowing that his life depended on his doing exactly as he was told, Smith opened the door more quietly than Fred himself could have done.

The basement was as silent as the rest of the building. It looked like a dungeon, with its gray brick walls, its stone floor, its naked light bulbs.

"Close the door."

Smith slid the grill shut.

Again Fred stopped, and listened for any sound of life. Nothing. Slowly, and with the gun in Smith's back, they started to walk along the stone-flagged corridors. There were metal drums against one wall. There were bags of cement. The various pipes and tubes that ran over the gray walls were painted light green and were dusty. They walked, Smith seeming scarcely to touch the ground with his feet, and Fred, just as he had never felt stronger, in spite of his burden, never having felt lighter.

There was a burglar alarm on the green iron service

117

door. Fred had to lay down Bob's body in order to turn it off. Then carefully and, oh, so quietly, he opened the lock on the door. But it gave him no difficulty. He was well trained and could open any door.

Leaving Bob lying where he was, the gun still in Smith's back—though hidden now in Fred's pocket—Fred stepped out into the night, pushing the boy in front of him.

The air made him feel light-headed for a second. How noisy the night was! How loud, and careless, and indifferent! The raucous wind, the roaring cars, even, it seemed, the high, heavy buildings and the thick black clouds in the sky, lit up every now and then by a trace of moon—how they all joined together to create a thunderous chorus; as if they had conspired together, like the privileged at a party in a land of misery, to drown out the sounds of horror drifting up from the street; the sounds of life. . . .

Then Fred pulled himself together. They had to walk up the first three steps before they could see down the street.

A man walking his dog appeared to be the only person about, and in spite of that first illusion of the noise of traffic, there was little actually on the street; most of it was coming from Central Park West and, farther off, from Columbus Avenue.

They waited for two minutes, until the dog-walker had disappeared, then they went back into the basement. Fred made Smith stand in front of him as he leaned down to pick up Bob's body again. Although Fred reckoned that the boy, if he had been clever, could have managed to push past him at that moment when both his hands were full with Bob, Smith still seemed too hypnotized, too frightened even to move unless he was told to, let alone to contemplate or attempt escape.

When Bob was over his shoulder again, they stepped

out once more into the night, and Fred told Smith to pull the door shut behind him. It had suddenly occurred to him that it would be better to return the stolen car and then go back to Brooklyn, rather than come back to this apartment when he had finished with Bob and Smith. Assuming everything went well, there was no point in running the risk, at the very end, of being caught sneaking in through the service entrance. The one small risk in going back to Brooklyn would be if the doorman should call up for some reason and not find him in. But that risk was infinitesimal.

He told Smith to check the street once more. The boy did, and then dumbly shook his head. Fred crouched back into the shadows on his hands and knees and motioned Smith to do the same. Again he reckoned that the boy, had he wanted to, could have run. But once again he didn't— he merely, hopelessly, obeyed.

They heard someone pass by on the other side of the street. Then two people. Then some cars. And then Smith, sent up again by Fred, nodded.

Fred walked quickly up the steps, crossed the sidewalk, opened the luggage door of the Ford, and shoved Bob's body inside. He motioned Smith into the passenger seat, and closed the door on him.

He got into the driver's seat, stretched across Smith to lock him in, and then leaned down and found the wires he had to connect to start the car.

It didn't take him long.

He drove slowly, and parked the car on the museum side of 79th Street. And now, for the first time since he had hit Bob, he started to feel just very slightly nervous. He would have to get Bob's body out of the car, into the park; he'd have to get Smith to cut Bob's throat, shoot the boy, and then get away, all without anyone seeing him. But was it possible? There were so many windows, so many eyes in the night; and what lovers might be around, or bums sleeping on benches? He sat still and watched the cars going past; and then, as if the gods had seen his doubt and wanted, for reasons of their own, to help him, a few drops of rain began to fall onto the windshield of the car. He watched them splatter on the glass, and prayed for more; and more came.

After two minutes it was raining heavily, and if there had been anyone in the park, they would surely have left by now. Fred got out of the car, opened the luggage door, pulled out Bob's body, lifted it onto his shoulder, and ran into the park—all, as far as he was aware, without breathing.

No voice shouted at him; no one tried to stop him.

He dropped Bob's body in a dark corner by the side entrance to the museum, then ran back to the car and got in. Smith's eyes were staring at him. He unlocked the boy's handcuffs, took them off, and put them in his pocket. He pulled the tape off the thin, weak mouth. Then he took Bob's gun out of his pocket, waited for a couple of cars to pass, and whispered, "Come on. Get out."

Smith got out and stood on the wet sidewalk; a pathetic creature who liked to be mistreated, soaking in the rain.

Fred walked with him to where he had dropped Bob's body, and took the bread knife from his pocket. He handed it to Smith, who took it without a word. Fred said softly, "Okay, then. Cut his throat."

Smith stared at him and didn't move.

Fred repeated, "Cut his throat."

"No," Smith whispered.

Fred held the gun up to the boy's head.

"No," Smith said again. "I can't. I've never killed anyone."

"Well, you're going to now."

"No."

"Do you want me to help you?"

"No."

"It'll be quite easy. You just pull the knife hard across his throat, once."

Smith started to cry. "Please."

Fred whispered, "If you don't cut his throat, I'll kill you."

"And if I do?" the boy sobbed.

"Then I'll let you go. You'll just be the Cop Killer on the run again. You'll be free."

"No. Please," Smith whined yet again.

"You'll be free," Fred repeated.

Somewhere a tree groaned in the storm. It was a horrible noise. It seemed to come from Bob himself. . . .

And then Smith did something surprising. Without saying another word, without a moment's hesitation, he dropped to his knees beside Bob, who was lying face down, picked up his head by its dark, fine hair, ripped the bread knife across the throat with a savagery that Fred would have thought him incapable of, threw down the knife, and then stood up and faced Fred with a look of hatred and, almost, pride. He was quivering.

Fred stared down at Bob. Smith had almost severed his head. He stared down at Bob, then up at the boy, down again at Bob, and then, suddenly, wanted to vomit. And then he remembered what he had to do. He lifted the gun, pointed it at Smith's head, and squeezed the trigger.

The gun clicked.

It wasn't loaded. Compassionate Bob, when he had come to the apartment to take Smith in, had been afraid of accidents and hadn't loaded his gun. The gun wasn't loaded. The gun wasn't loaded. . . . In the second after he had so uselessly squeezed the trigger, all these thoughts went through Fred's mind. He stood there, paralyzed, staring at the useless piece of metal in his hand.

But that little click, that quiet, inoffensive noise, so small amid the tumult of a windy, rainy night on the island of Manhattan, had a different effect on Smith. He who had been hypnotized, who like a priest in a trance of ecstasy had cut the throat of a human sacrifice, was transformed by that tiny click. He was awakened from his trance. He was released from his holy duties. He gave one terrible glance at Fred, as if he had never seen him before or had only just recognized him, and then turned and started to run.

Fred hesitated. What should he do? Throw the gun down beside Bob? No. Bob's prints weren't on it. There was no point. Should he follow Smith? Run after him, shouting, "Stop, killer," and say he had seen the boy in the park but had arrived just too late to save Bob's life? Bob had already been dead, the autopsy would show—but that simply meant that Smith had killed him earlier. In any case, he would have caught the Cop Killer. But if Smith told the truth—told all about the apartment? If—

He floundered about within himself, a big man lost in the vast dark apartment of his own consciousness, trying, as it were, to find the lights.

And then he did. He knew that he had to catch Smith. He started to run. He had to catch the boy before anyone else did.

But if he caught him they would surely be seen, the two of them. And then when Bob's body was found . . . He was running, but he was stumbling with confusion. He didn't know what to do; but he knew what he wanted to do. He wanted to howl a curse out into the night; a curse on Smith, and a curse on Bob; a curse on all the forces of chaos and guilt that had broken into his ordered world, and had destroyed it. Oh, why hadn't they left him alone in the lovely formal garden of his life? Why had they burst in and tried to touch him, Bob with his so-called humanity, and Smith with his madness? Why hadn't they left him alone in his coldness and his isolation and his lonely passion?

He thought he was running fast, but he hardly seemed to have moved. He was still in the park. And there was Smith, running up the street toward Central Park, a thin boy in a black cap, with a scarf flapping around his neck. He had to catch hi—

He stopped abruptly. There was someone—a man, it looked like—walking along the sidewalk toward Smith. Fred stood still and watched. The boy was running. Would he stop whoever it was and ask for help? He was almost upon the man. And then, involuntarily, Fred winced. Smith, in his panic, obviously hadn't seen the man. He had crashed right into him. He half fell. And then—then he picked himself up and started running again.

The man stood still and looked after him; looked after him, and then seemed to be staring at his hand.

Fred, very slowly, backed into the shadows, went back into the dark angle where Bob lay with his gaping throat.

He stayed there until the man, hurrying along again now—glad, obviously, that nothing worse than the rain and a collision had happened to him—had gone past. He stayed there for five minutes. For ten minutes. Because he couldn't catch Smith now. Smith had gotten away. Everything was over. Everything. The destruction of his life was complete. He stood there in the rain, with the water pouring down his face, and thought of his father, and his mother; of his ugly, wretched childhood. He thought of all the cruelty and sadness of life. He thought of all the illusions, all the vain hopes, all the useless dreams. He thought of Bob, who had been the youngest son of a large family who had adored him, and whom he had adored; a man who had been as aware of misery as Fred himself, but who had thought that it could be made bearable, even transformed into something good, by pity; a man who had thought that suffering, weak humanity should be helped, not realizing—or perhaps, yes, realizing, but not allowing himself to admit—that by stooping to help, by stretching out a helping hand, he would eventually be pulled down himself. Oh, why hadn't he realized that? Fred thought. As Fred stood there, he realized he was crying; crying for himself, and for Bob, and for the whole sad world. He was even crying, he realized, for Smith.

And then, because he had never, as far as he recalled, cried like that in his life before, and no longer caring who saw him or what happened to him, and feeling, strangely, glad that everything was over—that he no longer had to abide by any rules; that he could finally relax, and no longer had to be strong—he walked out of the park, went to the stolen car, drove it back to where he had found it (the gods, the ironical gods, had left him his parking space), slammed the door, walked down to the subway, took the train to Brooklyn, went back to his small shabby apartment, and fell asleep.

Next morning when he woke he decided he would go to Central Park West and wait for someone to fetch him there. At least, he thought, let him be found amid the ruins of his kingdom; let him have the bitter satisfaction of seeing them laugh at him, of seeing them jeer at his so-called madness and at his big empty soul.

He stopped briefly at a newsstand to read the headlines of the papers—"Another Slaying," "Seventh Policeman Killed"—and what was written, in only slightly smaller print, underneath—"Killer Collides with Passerby," "Killer Puts Bloody Hands on Passerby"—but he didn't bother to buy one. There was no point.

That they would come to him, he had no doubt at all. Smith, he reckoned, if he wasn't recognized and arrested within twenty-four hours, would give himself up within a few days. A week, maybe. Even ten days. But not much longer.

Should he call in sick, he wondered, or just disappear, and wait? He didn't know, and couldn't decide. On the one hand, it was as pointless to call in as it would have been to buy a newspaper; on the other hand, why not make this last formal gesture before leaving the dance forever?

He debated with himself as he rode up in the elevator, and then he called. He said he had hepatitis and the doctor had told him to stay in bed for about a month. This morning there were no laughing comments; his sickness was accepted without a word. Bob's death was the only event of importance.

"Yes," Fred said in a soft voice, he had heard. He couldn't bring himself to say anything more.

When he had hung up he called Bob's number, not expecting any reply. But Lenore herself answered. He murmured that he was sorry, and she said that she was too, sort of. She sounded, Fred thought, as sharp and revoltingly slick as ever. But then he told himself that he was no longer in a position to make such judgments and that everyone's reaction to tragedy was different, and he added, "If I can do anything for you—"

"Thank you," Lenore whispered. Then, snappily, "Like what?"

"I don't know," Fred said. "Anything."

"Thank you," Lenore repeated. "I'll let you know, Fred. Goodbye."

"Goodbye," Fred said.

He was about to hang up when he heard that Lenore hadn't. And she didn't for almost a minute. But she didn't say anything more. She simply cried. And as Fred listened to her, with his eyes closed, the sound of her weeping somehow relieved him, made him feel almost happy. And when at last the line did go dead, he asked himself if the reason for this could be that he, Fred O'Connor, felt guilty. Was it possible . . . ?

He changed into his fine clothes—how stupid they were; they were just clothes, like any others—and went into the living room. He poured himself a glass of whiskey and sat down. After a while he stood up again and looked out the window. It was the beginning of spring. A wind still bent the trees in the park and billowed under coats and skirts, and the sky wasn't as clear and blue as it had been during the period—how long ago had it been?—when Smith was his prisoner and he had thought that everything was set for life. But the clouds were white, and there was a quickness in the air, and the park was obviously about to burst into green.

But, Fred thought, this spring would never come through his windows, never come into his blood. His seasons were over. Now all that was left to him was the dry sterile time between now and when the doorbell rang and they came to take him away.

He sat down again.

Let it be soon, he thought.

He sat there all day, not exactly sleeping, or thinking, or doing anything. He simply sat there, and became his room, and didn't even finish the one glass of whiskey he had poured himself.

At eight o'clock he went into the kitchen and opened some tins and ate a sort of dinner; he didn't bother to throw away the tins afterward, or to wash his knife and fork and plate, or to wipe up the oil that had spilled out of the tin of tuna fish when he opened it. Not only was there no point in doing so, but also he decided that he preferred that there be a mess when they came to find him. It would satisfy them more. Because that way they would never be able to imagine the order there had been. . . .

At about ten o'clock he lay down on the floor and fell asleep.

At eleven he was awakened by the doorbell.

So, he thought, as he got slowly to his feet, glanced at his watch, and straightened his tie, he hadn't had to wait long. Not even a day. Well—he guessed he was glad. . . .

He walked slowly, but without hesitating, down the corridor to the hallway. Then he straightened his tie once more and opened the door.

He didn't know who or what he had expected. Although he hadn't let himself think about the specifics, he was still taken aback to see—not two or three uniformed men—but simply a pale, frightened-looking boy with a shaven head. A weak, wretched-looking boy whose name—it was as if he recognized him from some police dossier, or had seen his photograph in the paper, but had never had anything to do with him personally—was Leo Smith. He neither knew what to make of it, nor what to do.

He stood there in his gray silk suit and his monogrammed shirt, a big red man with the manner of an old maid, and murmured, "Smith."

The boy looked at Fred as if he too only recognized Fred from some secondary source, and then whispered, "Can I come in?"

Fred stood back, let the boy in, and closed the door behind him. Only then did he manage to take in what had happened. It was Smith who stood there in his hallway! Pale, perverted Smith, who had been his prisoner! The trembling boy who had savagely cut Bob's throat last night, and run away from him. And now he had come back to him. Had come home, as it were.

Smith was staring at him, waiting. For what? To be hit? To be killed on the spot?

Fred walked away. He walked back down the corridor to the living room and sat down. What did it mean? He closed his eyes and tried to think of an explanation. But when he couldn't, he opened them again, saw that he was alone, and called softly, "Smith."

The boy walked nervously into the living room. His teeth were chattering now. He seemed about to burst into tears. He said miserably, "No one saw me come here, I don't think. I slipped past the doorman again. Like I did when I first came here."

Fred said nothing.

"I'm sorry. But I didn't know where else to go. I've been walking in the park for hours. And riding the subway. I threw away my cap. I didn't know what to do. So I thought I'd come back here. I couldn't go on any longer. You don't mind, do you? If they'd caught me, I'd have had to tell them about you. About here. I—" And then he did burst into tears.

Fred watched him; watched him as if he were watching a seal who was performing odd tricks.

Smith didn't attempt to wipe his eyes, or to sit down, or to move at all; he simply stood there with his hands hanging at his sides, and let the tears pour from his red pale eyes, down over his cheeks, and onto his jacket and his sweater and onto the floor.

And Fred didn't move either. His first thought was that if the boy hadn't been seen coming here, then everything was as it had been before; exactly as it had been before. His hope, his future, his life had risen like the proverbial phoenix from the ashes, and recreated themselves. His second thought was that nothing was as it had been before. On the surface—yes, maybe. But nothing could be trusted any more. Were his life and his future in fact safe still? Or was the appearance of preservation only an illusion, an ironical mirage?

As he sat there watching the crying boy, the second thought gained ground over the first in Fred's mind, and slowly displaced it altogether. No, he told himself, nothing was as before. And the appearance of safety mustn't be trusted. For one thing, after Smith had run away last night, and after he had given up hope of catching him, he had walked to the stolen car without trying to hide. Someone must have seen him then, even if he hadn't been seen before. And when it was discovered that Bob had been killed before he had had his throat cut, and killed someplace other than where he had had his throat cut, then surely someone would come forward and say they had seen a big man walking out of the park. A big man who had gotten into a blue Ford and driven away. Then probably the owner of the blue Ford, finding that someone had used his car—because he hadn't really done much to hide the wires he had pulled out to start it—would come forward. And as the car had been parked right outside the service entrance to his building, no doubt the doormen would be questioned. And they would say, "Sure, there's a big man who lives here. And a few weeks ago a youth wearing a black cap, whose name—" they might even remember his name—"was Leo Smith, came around asking for him." Leo Smith . . . and then, if they didn't come right upstairs and find them both, they would go to Leo's grandmother, and she would tell them about his visit. She would give them a minute description of him. And then they would know.

All this was one reason why nothing was the same as it had been. But it was not the main reason. Because there were a great many if's and but's in all this, and it was equally possible that no one had seen him; that the owner of the blue Ford would think only that some kids had vandalized his car; and that no questions would be asked about him or Smith. Besides, there were a lot of people who wore woolen caps, and a lot of people called Smith. Fred had never had the boy sent up, so as far as anyone knew there was no connection between them.

No, the main reason why his apparent safety could not be trusted was that Fred felt he himself had changed. Something had happened to him. Before, he had had his dream of a world as a formal dance, in which every step was preordained and planned; where good was the perfect execution of the dance; and where the only sin was to question the why's and wherefore's of the movements. But now, for some reason, he felt himself questioning not merely the why's and wherefore's but the reasons for the dance itself. It wasn't exactly that he had lost his dream, but rather that, for the first time, he had become aware of its limits, the frontiers that stood between it and—nothingness. Before, he had always thought of it and believed it to be infinite, a perfect, curved dream. . . .

He watched the tears from Smith's eyes fall onto the carpet, and then, only very slightly disapprovingly, he cleared his throat.

"You can stay if you want to," he said slowly. "But you don't have to."

Smith looked at him through his tear-filled eyes, apparently not understanding him.

"You see," Fred went on, "Bob was already dead when you cut his throat."

CHAPTER 8

As soon as he had said it, Fred realized that he shouldn't have; he was depressed, shocked, disturbed, and one should never do anything unless one was absolutely calm. But he had said it, and the effect on Smith was immediate.

First the boy sat down on the floor, as heavily as if he had been pushed. Then, after he had gone on sniveling for a while, he wiped his nose with the back of his hand and gave Fred a look that was both ashamed and accusative. And finally, after another two minutes, he gave one of his social smiles and started to speak in his flattest, most *casual* voice.

"Well, that's good," he said. "I guess I should have realized. Perhaps I did. But I was too frightened to really know what I was doing." Then he positively beamed at Fred. "Not that it makes any difference, of course. I mean technically, morally, let's say, I'm still guilty of murder. Because since I *did* think he was still alive, and I cut his throat—" Smith shrugged. There was spittle at the corners of his mouth.

Fred stared at the boy, horrified, sickened. Just a few minutes ago he had been sniveling, crying, flinging himself on his mercy. But he had simply been crying with fear —with all the despair of a small boy who has been playing an evil game which has finished badly, and who wants everyone to reassure him, and bundle him up, and tell him that of course he wasn't doing anything wrong and that it wasn't his fault. He couldn't believe it. In spite of all that had happened, this was still a game for the boy. Fred also realized that strangely, suddenly—in spite of the fact that Smith was up here in his secret kingdom, in his prison— the power, the control of the situation, had been taken from him and had passed to this weak wretched boy with his smooth voice and smug manner. Yes, Smith had come back up to his prison, but Smith was no longer the prisoner. He, Fred O'Connor, was. And because the boy had so oddly, inexplicably, taken over, Fred felt he was bound to talk to him and to pretend to take him seriously; pretend that he didn't hear his smugness; pretend that he didn't realize all this was a game.

He said, "You're not technically or morally responsible for anything. I was pointing a gun at your head."

"I should have let you shoot," Smith purred. "Anyway, no one would ever believe the truth if I told it. I'd be arrested as your accomplice."

"Oh, they'd believe it all right. They'd come here and see all this; and your grandmother could probably get you acquitted of murdering the President, with all her money."

This seemed to annoy Smith. "No, she couldn't," he said sulkily. "Anyway, even if they didn't get me for killing your friend Bob, they'd probably get me for all the others."

Fred sighed. "Don't start that again. You know you've never killed anyone. You told me last night."

"I only said that because I didn't want to kill your friend. That was *real* last night. All the others were fantasies. I don't like to kill in reality."

Fred felt himself flushing. He wanted to scream, or to

get up and hit the boy. He couldn't stand it. All this flippant playing around with words, all this repulsive play-acting.

"What are you planning to do?" he said.

"Well, I guess I better stay here and hide out for a while. If that's okay with you." He smiled at Fred again. "I guess you better, too. Just in case anyone saw you last night." He stood up, walked across the room, and sat, sprawling, in the other armchair. "Christ, I'm tired," he drawled. "I didn't sleep at all last night."

"Aren't you scared that I'll tie you up again?" Fred said. "Or even kill you?"

"No. Not really. There's no point in tying me up, is there? After all, I'm not about to go out and risk getting arrested. You couldn't kill me, because you'd have to get rid of my body somewhere. And when it was found, Grandmother would remember your visit." He laughed, oh, so casually. "You should have thought of that last night when you pulled that gun on me. They'd have got you."

Fred flushed again. "Yes," he murmured. "I should have. I didn't think."

Once more Smith laughed. "To tell the truth, neither did I until a short time ago."

Fred whispered, miserably, "They'll find me—us—anyway, quite soon. I've been much too careless. They're bound to find some clue. Footprints, your fingerprints on the knife, someone who saw me getting Bob's body out of the car."

"Yes, I guess," Smith said. He didn't sound interested. "Did you work today?"

"No. I called in sick. I said I had hepatitis. I said I'd be sick for a month."

"That was dumb. That'll make them suspect you, if they don't already."

"Why?"

"Going sick the day your buddy gets killed."

"He wasn't my buddy. I almost never spoke to him except when we were here." Then he lowered his voice and muttered huskily, "Do you think they do suspect me?"

Smith looked concerned now, as if he were speaking to a child. "Sure they do. They must. They must suspect everybody. But *you*—" He grinned condescendingly.

"Of all the killings?" Fred whispered.

"Yes. Probably."

"No," Fred said, firmly now. "They couldn't. They have no reason to."

Smith raised his eyebrows. "Well, we'll see, anyway." Then he frowned. "By the way, what about the doormen here?"

"I don't know." Fred shrugged. "But I hope they won't remember your asking for me and giving your name, if anyone comes around asking questions."

Smith opened his eyes wide now in mock astonishment. "I wasn't thinking about that. I meant about your friend Bob. They're bound to see his name and his photograph in the paper or on television."

Fred lay back in his chair and closed his eyes. He wanted to sleep.

"Don't tell me you didn't think about that?"

"No," Fred whispered. "I didn't."

Smith laughed. "My God, you're efficient!"

"Maybe," Fred said, "the photograph in the papers, if they have one, will be an old one. Or a bad one. And if there's only the name, maybe they won't associate it with Bob. After all, they didn't know he was a cop, and wouldn't think he was, living here. And he didn't come that often."

"He came last night."

"Maybe," Fred said desperately, "none of them read any newspapers." Then he asked slowly, "Why did you come back here, if you thought—?"

Smith gazed at Fred, and then nodded. "You've changed. You know that. I do believe you feel guilty about killing that guy." Then he shrugged. "I guess the only thing we can do is wait and hope that if the doormen do recognize the photograph they won't say anything to anyone. There's no reason why they should, in fact. I mean, they might say they're sorry to you, but they don't know that this apartment is a secret, do they? They probably think everyone knows about it. And if Bob only came here every now and then, they wouldn't think he lived here, would they? I mean—he didn't, anyway. They'd just think that he visited occasionally. Or that you let him have a key."

What was the boy trying to do? Reassure him, or sow more doubts in his mind than there already were? Fred didn't know. He repeated, "Why did you come here?"

"Because I couldn't think where else to go," Smith said, "and I was scared." His honesty, Fred guessed, was meant to be disarming. But somehow, while he believed him, he also believed that the boy had come back because he wanted to see, for better or worse, the end of the drama or game or whatever it was, and knew that that end wouldn't be too long in coming.

But when, and how?

He fell asleep asking himself these questions, only hearing as if from the far distance Smith's voice saying flatly, "The only thing we can do is wait, and hope."

They waited for a week; and if total silence from the outside world was a good sign—which Fred guessed it was—their hope was justified.

They did nothing all day except think. At least Fred thought, and he guessed Smith did, too. But he didn't ask and didn't want to know. Their conversation was kept to a minimum, with only the occasional "Do you want to eat now?" or "Where do you keep the toilet tissue if there is any more?" to break the quiet. The first day, Smith had tried to talk to Fred, asking him about his family, about his religious beliefs, about his past; but since none of his questions had received a reply he had given up and now simply sat in the kitchen listening to the radio—until Fred said that that irritated him and smashed it. He didn't want anything to disturb his thoughts.

For the first few days he simply thought about being found out and arrested and sent to prison for life. And then, as it started to seem that maybe he wouldn't be, he thought about his life as it had been up to now. Then he thought about what would happen if he were never found out, but simply had to remain Smith's prisoner forever. Then he thought that he had been stupid not to have bought at least a couple of beds; he was stiff and sore from sleeping on the floor. More and more, especially as he was falling asleep and when he first woke up in the morning, he thought about Bob.

On the morning of the seventh day, when he awoke with the green-brown carpet tickling his nostrils and the gray dawn light making the living room soft and flabby and suffocating, he couldn't bear it any more. It was ironic, he realized, but he craved Bob's pity; he would even have traded the apartment for Bob and the very qualities that had made him despise Bob when he was alive. He had to know why Bob had pitied him. He had to. Perhaps Bob had spoken to Lenore about him.

He decided to call her, as he lay on the floor of the dawn-gray living room; but by the time he had gotten up, showered, shaved, and made himself some coffee, he wasn't so sure. And by the time Smith—who slept in the corridor—walked into the kitchen with his usual "Hi, good morning," as if he owned the place, Fred had almost definitely decided not to.

If only, he thought, he could recapture the strength that had been taken from him; if only he could regain his dream intact. . . .

He said, "You know who Bob was married to?"

"No." Smith smiled, as if, there never having been an announcement of the impending marriage in the social column of the Sunday *Times,* he couldn't possibly have known. "Although," he went on, "he did say something about her when he burst into the bathroom last week. But I was too shocked—I didn't know what was going on—to really understand. I was meaning to ask you, but I forgot. Something about a letter."

Fred nodded. "There were some articles about the police once in some magazine, written by a woman called Lenore Morris. You wrote her a letter which she never answered. Your grandmother told me."

"And she"—what wonders there were in social life, Smith's eyes seemed to say—"was married to that Bob?"

"Yes."

"Well!" Smith smiled again, with just a trace of embarrassment. "It's a small world, isn't it?"

Fred shrugged.

"And she read about my disappearance in the paper, and your friend put two and two together."

"Yes."

"Do you think," Smith said, "that he said anything to her? About me?"

"No. I'm sure he didn't."

"What's she like?"

"You read her articles."

"Yes. They impressed me at the time." A casual laugh. "I guess I might find them rather superficial now. I mean—I've gone rather beyond her, haven't I? I can just picture her though. I bet she's small and sharp." He snapped his fingers. "And she probably deep down had wild erotic dreams about being screwed or tortured by cops, which she jokes about to all her friends, who admire her for her frankness, but which she can't quite pass off to herself. So she compromised and married that lemon and kidded herself that she loved him for his integrity."

"Shut up!" Fred said. He felt slightly shocked. "That's you you're talking about, not Lenore."

"Oh, I'm *sorry*, sir," Smith mocked. "I didn't realize."

Fred told himself he mustn't get angry. He mustn't. He must accept everything. He murmured, "I was thinking of going to see her."

"Don't," Smith ordered, suddenly serious. "If you go see her you'll give yourself away."

"No I won't."

"Yes you would. I told you. You've changed. Something's happened to you. I bet you're just longing to go and cry on her shoulder, and tell her you killed her husband, and ask for her forgiveness."

"No," Fred murmured.

"Then why?" How arrogant the boy was; how cold those watery eyes that had always seemed so weak. . . .

"Because—" He stopped. How could he say, "Because I want to know why Bob pitied me"? How could he say it even to himself? He shrugged. "I don't know. I guess I just want to see if she's all right. Tell her I'm sorry."

"For what?"

"For Bob's being dead." He bowed his head. "But maybe you're right. It's better not to go."

"You'll give yourself away if you do." Smith turned on the coffee grinder, as if to underscore his point. "You really *have* changed, you know. You're falling to pieces."

Fred looked at the white monkey-hand holding the dark plastic grinder. He muttered, "Well, that's what you came back to see, isn't it?"

Smith turned off the grinder. "Possibly," he said. "But I

don't think so. I was really just scared, and coming back here was sort of instinctive."

Fred wandered back into the living room and looked out the window at the park. It was visibly spring now. But how right he had been to think that this spring would never come through the glass, never come into the apartment or his life. It was like looking at a photograph. And how much he *had* changed, to care about such things. . . . He turned away and called to Smith, "I think I'm going out, anyway. I guess it's safe. I think I'll go to Brooklyn and check if there's any mail."

Smith came to the door of the living room and looked at him like a father considering whether to give a child permission to go out. Fred waited apprehensively, knowing that if Smith said no he wouldn't disobey him. But the boy, after inspecting him long enough, with just the right degree of contempt, shrugged. "I guess you can," he said.

How warm it was! How soft the wind! How gentle and peaceful and lovely! It was like a poet's description of spring. As he walked slowly toward the subway, Fred thought how temporary the massive buildings around him seemed now. Only a week or so ago they had seemed so solidly, so monumentally set. Half-crossing his eyes, he visualized Manhattan's skyscrapers as they seemed to him today—temporary, and fragile, and almost touchingly tacky, as if they might at any moment be blown away, like tents laid out in rows on sand.

How very beautiful it was! And yet, Fred told himself, opening his eyes again wide and looking at the cars, and the sidewalk, and the uniformed doormen hovering under the awnings, how sad it was, too. How sad that he could only look, and imagine, and not participate. How sad that only now could he feel that the world around him was not something to be mastered, conquered, and beaten back, but something to be lived with, and through—like an ocean of seemingly chaotic currents, where one had to live within the general drift and pull and pattern of the waves, but in which it was also possible to swim, as it were, one's own strokes. How sad that only now, now that he was dead, he should become aware of life. . . .

This sadness, and the feeling of being dead, stayed with him all the time he was on the subway, and hit him with even greater force when, carrying two letters that he had taken from his mailbox, he opened the door of his apartment—his real apartment, it suddenly struck him as being. Before, only the apartment on Central Park West had seemed real, but now—oh, he suddenly loved this place! This long thin living room with its bare boards, pale grubby green walls and odd ugly furniture that he had picked up in the street. This small peeling bedroom with its mattress lying on the floor on an old worn rug. This tiny, hideous kitchen, painted orange and green and blue by the former tenants, with its old stained sink and stove that had only been cleaned once or twice, and where, at night, roaches grazed. Why had he never since he had taken this place, when Helen left him, thought of it as home? What was wrong with it? Sure, the building was shabby, but it too had a view of a park—a view he had never looked at, of a park he had never walked in—and it too provided him with all he needed: a roof over his head, a place to sleep and a place to wash and cook in. What else did he need? What else had he ever needed? Oh *why* had he had that dream? But it was no use asking why now. It was too late. He had had his dream, and it had been with him too long—all his life perhaps—to be shaken off now. Now all that was left him was an empty apartment, and a mad boy, and dust.

If only, Fred thought as he sat down heavily on the

edge of his gray, unmade mattress, he could have gone to see Lenore and talk. If only he could talk to anyone as he had talked to Bob that day in the bar on Avenue B. But Smith had said no, and Smith, now, for as long as it lasted, was leading the game. And the boy had been right, of course. If he had gone to Lenore, he probably would have broken down and told her what he had done. Sooner or later he would have told her everything. And in spite of the change he had felt come over him, he didn't want to. He didn't want to go to prison. He didn't want to be tried, and condemned, and locked up. He just wanted to be left alone with the consciousness of his own death, and to hope that the awareness of what might have been might give the dust in his mouth at least the taste of life.

But he would have liked to talk to someone. . . .

He opened the first of his two letters and threw it away with only a glance; it was some sort of circular. But when he opened the second letter he started to tremble and, involuntarily, to smile. There was, perhaps, some hope! There was, perhaps, some chance of his regaining some share, some tiny share, in the real, living world. Because the letter started, "Dear Fred, I have to talk to you," and ended with the signature of Lenore.

What came in between read:

I came up to find you—I heard you were sick—but no one answered the door. I hope you aren't dead. [There was a word heavily crossed out in ink after "dead." It looked like "too."] I have to talk to you about Bob. I have suddenly realized, after a relationship of almost four years and a marriage of a year and a half, that I didn't know him. And I have to. I have to find out so that I can get some sort of order and sense back into my existence and put our relationship in its proper context. If I don't, I'm never going to get over—not his death; I guess I'll never get over that—but his *life*, and our life together. It'll torment me forever. You might think it strange that I ask

141

you, but it was you who introduced us, and I know that for some reason you played a significant part in Bob's life. I can't think what, or how, or why, but you did—and I must know. Please, as soon as you get this, call me. I shall be at home. I'm trying, while I can still remember the exact texture of Bob's skin, the exact smell of him as he slept, the exact way he moved his lips when he spoke, the exact way he stood when he was happy, mad, serious, silly, to write everything down; to see if I can find out what I didn't know by recreating the appearance, both exterior and interior, of Bob. I want to batter my soul with pain as if it were an atom, and when it explodes I hope that the energy it releases will give me the power to possess entirely after Bob's death what I never possessed entirely during his life, and thereby let Bob live forever, and meaningfully, with a purpose, a sense, in me.

That's the real thing that bothers me, I think. Not only is Bob's death meaningless to me still, but, at the moment, so is his life, and our marriage. I can't let four great, happy years of my life be meaningless. I must recreate Bob whole, and thereby make me whole. And to do this I must know what I have, a feeling only you can tell me. I have dreamed about you every night since Bob died, and you're like a great dark presence standing between him and me. *Please* get in touch with me as soon as you can. I'm sorry I didn't say all this to you when you called, but I couldn't think then, and besides, it hadn't really hit me. I thought I'd see you at the funeral and speak to you then, but that was when I heard you were sick. I hope you're better now.

Fred read the letter through twice, and then put it down on the bed beside him and simply stared at it. If he had received such a letter ten days ago, he would have laughed with derision and torn it up; told himself that only someone like Lenore would want to make copy out of her husband's death, would be preoccupied only with her own reaction to that death, never really sparing a thought or a regret for the man himself. But now—though the letter did still reek of the Lenore he had always despised—he felt warmed by it, touched by it, and grateful for it. Even the slickness of it, the shallowness of it, and at one point—"to batter my soul with pain"—the downright falseness of it only seemed to make the letter as a whole more genuine, more desperate, more truly a cry of grief, made more tragic by the fact that Lenore, with all her literary training and background, was incapable of expressing it. The words were what they were, but the feeling behind them—that was genuine. He was sure. It had to be. Oh, let it be, he whispered silently to himself.

Putting Smith, and the apartment, and all that had happened and was happening still out of his mind, he went to the telephone and dialed Lenore's number.

"Yes," Lenore said.

"Hi. It's Fred."

"Hi." She sounded as if she couldn't think why in the world he was calling. For some reason, Fred was glad of her attitude. It was like having his face washed with an astringent. It woke him up. It made him attentive.

"I got your letter," he went on. "I'm sorry I haven't called before, but I only just got home. I've got a mild attack of hepatitis, and I went to stay with my sister for a week."

"I didn't know you had a sister."

"There's no reason you should," Fred said, feeling pleased with this answer. It was the sort of retort Lenore herself would have made. "The doctor told me I should stay in bed for a month, but I got bored. And I'm feeling better now. I feel tired the whole time, and I'm only eating boiled rice, but I've never been sick in my life, and I'm not aiming to start now."

"That's good."

Lenore was waiting for him to get back to the subject of the letter. But he wasn't about to. It was she who had asked him to call. He waited.

"Fred?"

"Yeah, I'm here."

There was another long pause. Then: "Well, when can I see you?"

"Whenever you like."

"I guess you couldn't come here, could you? I know I should come and see you if you're sick, but I don't like to go out unless it's absolutely necessary."

Did she not believe he was sick? Fred wondered. Or did she simply believe that her sensibility was more delicate than his health, however sick he was?

He said, "I guess I can make it to the Village."

"Maybe you should take a cab," Lenore said grandly.

Was she, Fred wanted to ask, planning to reimburse him for the fare and put it down to research expenses?

He said, "Yeah, I probably will."

"When will you be here?"

"I'll come right away."

He went right away; and it was only when he was in the cab that he realized that not only had he not thought about the possibility of being watched or even arrested as he went in and out of his apartment, but also that, when he had agreed to go over to Lenore's, he hadn't for an instant worried about the danger of giving himself away to her. But it was she who wanted something from him, she who had asked to see him. And as long as she didn't know that he wanted something from her, too, then he was in no danger. What was more, he told himself, he intended to stay out of danger. Because now that he felt that he did have a chance of life, he was more than ever determined not to jeopardize that chance or to risk spending the life he might finally achieve in a prison cell.

It would be perfect, he thought, if Smith would get bored with him, would forget that he had ever met him, would go and tell someone else that he was the Cop Killer and had killed them all, including Bob. It would be so, so perfect. . . . And then he, Fred O'Connor, would quit the police, sell the apartment on Central Park West, and— go away. Leave New York. Even leave America, maybe. Perhaps he would go to Europe. Or even farther away. To India perhaps. To settle down somewhere and work with his hands. Yes, he would become a carpenter or something, and marry some woman who had survived an ice age herself, and understood his scars—or one who was warm and temperate enough to coax some buds out of the shattered earth. Yes . . . And then they might have some children. He would like children. . . . Children he could bring up to be free and happy. Children he could love. Children he would never lecture to, never, ever. Unless, he thought, he decided to warn them of the dangers, of the mortal dangers, of committing themselves to dreams—to cold, dead dreams. . . .

And then, finally, he realized that just by getting into a taxi and giving the driver Lenore's address he had found out what he wanted to know. He realized that Lenore didn't have to tell him anything; or rather, that she had told him everything just by asking him to come. He realized, at last what Bob—unconsciously maybe, instinctively maybe, but certainly, for him, fatally—had pitied him for. . . .

Lenore, in a pink sweater set and pearls and a pair of faded old jeans, opened the door without a smile.

"My God, you look dreadful," she said. "You make me feel guilty."

Did he look dreadful, Fred wondered, or was it just that Lenore expected him to look dreadful and therefore saw him so? He didn't feel dreadful; what he had realized in the taxi had made him feel more at ease with himself than he could remember ever having felt in his life. In fact, when he had gotten out of the cab in front of the pink three-story house on Jane Street where Lenore lived, and had cast an eye around for the freaks, the faggots, the artists and the pseudo-artists he had always believed haunted the Village exclusively, he had been almost sorry not to see anyone except for a middle-aged couple carrying bags of groceries. He would have liked to test himself, to look at those people he had always considered to be the despicable, self-conscious ragtag of a guilty society, and to feel neither threatened by them, nor fearful of them, nor superior to them. Though there weren't any of them about, he had felt sure that he would have passed his test perfectly.

And while he had never felt more at ease, he had never, either, felt that he had to be more careful. As he stood there, massive, in Lenore's doorway, he had the distinct impression that this small, plump girl, in her efforts to give "meaning" to her life and to remove the "great dark presence" she felt standing between herself and her dead husband, would be only too glad to destroy him; to make a sacrifice of him in memory of Bob; or—by way of battering her soul with pain and getting some order and sense back into her existence—to cast the man who had introduced her to Bob in the role of the Cop Killer.

"Sit down," Lenore ordered. "D'you want some coffee?"

"No," Fred said. "I can't. I'll have a glass of water if you like."

As Lenore went over to the alcove where the sink and stove and refrigerator were, Fred lowered himself into a small, deep, battered old green armchair and looked around. No wonder Lenore could find no meaning in her years of cohabitation and marriage with Bob. There was no trace of him anywhere; no sign that he had ever lived in this tiny, menacing apartment that was, as far as Fred remembered, exactly the same as it had been five years ago. He always remembered that going into the damp, evil bathroom where the light didn't work, after they had made love and while he was wondering what it would be like to be married to her, had been one of the most disturbing, unaccountably frightening experiences of his life. He had never had such a clear, such a distinct vision of chaos. . . .

What was more, he thought as he took the glass of water from Lenore, this apartment—unlike his apartment in Brooklyn, which he had simply neglected and never cared for—could never have been made pleasant or even, really, habitable. What had Lenore and Bob *done* with all the money they earned? Had most of Bob's pay gone toward meeting his share of the expenses for the apartment on Central Park West, for that ball and chain Bob had worn around his ankle and been so loath—until the very end, when it was too late—to release himself from? No. It wasn't possible. Between them, they still must have been earning quite enough not to have to live in this place.

"Why did you and Bob never move from here?" he said.

"I wanted to, but years ago. Bob never did. He loved it here. And I'm sort of fond of it, in spite of everything. He said it was better to buy something in the country."

"Did you?"

"Yep. We signed the papers and put half the money down for an old farmhouse in Connecticut a couple of weeks ago."

How she relished the irony of it. . . .

Fred cleared his throat and murmured—quite gently, he heard, and without a trace of the primness that would have been in his voice a short while ago if he had said something similar—"What can I tell you about Bob, Lenore? You know we didn't really see that much of each other. I mean, I hardly knew him."

147

Lenore drummed her fingers on her faded knees. Her hands were as small and plump as the rest of her, and she had very long, unpainted nails. "Bob used to talk about you sometimes. But he used to think about you a lot more. He never said so. But I knew. And I want to know why."

"I don't know," Fred said.

"At times I got the real feeling that you—" she paused, and scratched at her elaborate-as-ever hairdo as she searched for the right way of putting it—"that you represented all the sins and sorrows of the world for him, and he felt he had to bear them on his back like Jesus with his damned cross."

"Bob felt that way about everyone."

"But why about you?"

"Maybe," Fred said, "it was something to do with how it all started. Maybe—you know—because of me telling Helen about— And then him marrying you and me getting divorced and—" He brought the words out cautiously.

"Oh, for Chrissake," Lenore snapped. "Apart from anything else, you and Helen got divorced before I even met Bob."

Fred shrugged. "Well, why didn't you ever ask him?"

"I did. He said he didn't know."

Fred smiled now. "Well, if he didn't know, I don't know why I should."

Lenore leaned over to her worktable, took a cigarette from an open pack, and lit it. She blew smoke out of her nostrils like an old actress.

"How long is this going to go on?" she said.

"What?"

"This cop killer going around. Bob told me before he died that they've got no idea, and now, with all the clues they have—"

"I don't know," Fred said. "I've been in bed since before Bob was killed, so I don't know what's going on. Besides, that's not really my department."

"They're not doing a goddamn thing. Apparently the guy the killer bumped into could only say he thought he was young, but he wasn't even sure about that. He said he thought his face was covered in some way. But he said he was too scared when he saw that there was blood on his hand to even look at who bumped into him. And then it rained all that night, so there were no footprints or anything, and the prints on the knife were all smudged, and—"

"Didn't anyone see anything from some window? They must have."

"They haven't in all the other cases, so I don't see why they should now. And I guess if anyone had seen anything, they'd be too scared to say. In case the maniac came calling on them."

Fred nodded thoughtfully.

Lenore shrugged. Then, returning suddenly to her former subject, she said scornfully, "You must know why Bob felt so damned sorry for you."

Fred thought he should be offended by her tone, but he smiled again and said, "Well, I'm sorry, I don't."

Lenore stared at him, as if making mental notes about his appearance; which, Fred guessed, she was doing. Then he added softly, "Maybe Bob thought I was—I dunno—unhappy, maybe."

"Everyone's unhappy."

"Oh," Fred said.

Then they sat and faced each other in silence for a while.

Finally Lenore asked, "You're not gay are you? You didn't have a thing about Bob?"

"No," Fred said.

"Lots of people did."

The silence returned.

This time Lenore broke it with: "You've changed, you know. I mean apart from the fact that you're sick." She scratched at her hair again, and laughed. "You've gotten sort of softer. I always used to think there was something hard and white and mad inside you. I don't see it any more."

"Well, thanks." Once more Fred smiled. "Perhaps that's why Bob felt sorry for me."

"Why do I dream about you, for God's sake? Why do I feel so sure you know something about Bob that I don't, and that you could tell me?"

Fred thought briefly of Smith's theory of Lenore's erotic fantasies. He shrugged.

"I just feel convinced that there's some sort of pattern I can't see. Some sort of clue that would make everything fall into place."

Fred, Bob, Lenore's articles about the police, Smith, Smith's disappearance, Lenore's telling Bob about it, Bob's death . . . Yes. There was a pattern. But Lenore would never find it. He was sure. He got up and said, "I'd better be going. I'm sorry I couldn't—" He smiled gently, for the last time.

"I'm sorry I dragged you all the way from Brooklyn for nothing."

"That's okay," Fred murmured. "I understand."

Lenore's eyes, just for a second, glittered with tears. Then she drew in hard on her cigarette, went over to the door, and opened it. "There's only one reason—one real reason—I can think of why Bob should have felt like he did about you," she said. "And that's because—" She hesitated. Then, looking up defiantly at Fred—how very small she was!—she ended, "You're not the Cop Killer, are you, Fred?"

Fred gazed at her for a while before replying, and now he didn't smile. "Why," he said at last, "are you always so fucking rude, Lenore?" Then, almost as an afterthought, he added, "But no. I'm not."

CHAPTER 9

"You went to see her, didn't you?" Smith said. "I know you did. And now she knows everything."

"No, she doesn't."

"Well, she will soon. Jesus, you're a fool."

Feeling more than ever like a small child being chastised by a strict parent, Fred stood in the long, dim corridor of the apartment and lowered his eyes in front of the now not quite shaven-headed boy. "There was a letter from her in Brooklyn asking me to go see her. I went. She's very unhappy."

"Everyone's unhappy."

"That's what she said."

Smith laughed.

"But it's not true," Fred said earnestly. "I'm not."

Smith stared at him, and just for a second there was, as there hadn't been for some time now, fear in his eyes. Then he laughed again. "That's 'cause you're mad."

Fred nodded.

"What have you got there?"

Fred looked at the brown paper bags in his arms. "Provisions," he said. "And a new bread knife."

Smith raised his eyebrows. With a coy, sarcastic smile, he asked, "What do you need a bread knife for? You always buy sliced bread."

Perhaps once he would have made a joke. But he didn't want to now, and especially not with Smith. He said simply, "Not always." And then: "I must go and put this stuff in the refrigerator."

As day followed day, Fred's wish that Smith would get tired and either go back to his grandmother's or vanish in a puff of smoke grew stronger and stronger in him. He figured that, now that he had changed, Smith was a sort of anomaly. The boy's presence, the fact that they were both more or less prisoners, the apartment itself, rather than irritating or disturbing or worrying Fred now, merely bored him. They had become superfluous, out of place, irrelevant.

Five days after his visit to Lenore he suggested that Smith stay on in the apartment for as long as he liked, and he would go back to Brooklyn, stay down there, and go back to work. But Smith, as he guessed he would, as he feared he would, said no.

"I'm not going to stay here by myself all day. I can't," the boy drawled. "I'd go out of my mind and end up calling the police and giving myself up. And you wouldn't want that, would you?"

"No," Fred answered. "But why don't you go back to your grandmother? I told you what Lenore said—the man you bumped into didn't even look at you, and they have no clues at all."

"That's what she said. I don't believe it. As soon as I got off the train in Providence they'd be waiting for me. And then they'd beat me up, and I wouldn't be able to stop myself from telling them where I'd been all this time and what I'd been doing. And you wouldn't want that, would you?" he repeated.

"No," Fred murmured, and left the room. There was no point in discussing the matter further. The boy obviously wanted to stay for reasons of his own, and since he had the upper hand, there was nothing he could do about it.

He wasn't entirely a prisoner, of course; Smith did let him go out sometimes—to buy food, to go to the bank, to buy him some clothes (underclothes, two pairs of dark trousers, five white shirts, some ties, a dark-blue blazer and some shoes), to buy a couple of portable beds and, because he no longer had the strength or the power to argue now, a radio and a television. But apart from that . . .

Fred bought nothing for himself, and he only bothered to shave and wash and change his own clothes because it gave him something to do. For the rest of the time he simply cooked, cleaned, and generally waited on the smartly dressed Smith, who stayed in the living room all day, watching old films on the television, occasionally asking Fred to bring him something.

He waited on the boy; he wondered how long this situation would go on, and how it would end. He also thought sometimes about Lenore and wondered how she was getting on in her attempt to give meaning to her late married life. Badly, he reckoned. After all, how could she cope unless she knew—unless he told her—what she wanted to know?

Poor Lenore . . .

He supposed it had all started with her. Or at least, the crack-up. If she hadn't come to interview him, he would never have made love with her, she would never have told Helen, he would never have gotten divorced. He would probably have spent his whole life being a prim, formal married man who happened to be a corrupt cop and who happened to have a secret apartment, but whose own little madnesses did little or no harm to anyone. And if she hadn't written her articles, or if Smith hadn't read them, maybe *his* particular form of madness would have taken another turn. The spoiled rich boy eager for experience might have been content simply to be whipped and beaten and remained, as his grandmother had so blandly put it, a masochist.

The thought of snappy little Lenore's hopeless quest to put her life in order, to find the pattern that she knew existed, worried him more and more, just as before he had gone to see her the thought of Bob's feeling sorry for him had worried him. Why did he care about her? he asked himself. Apart from right at the beginning—and even then it was doubtful—he had never liked her, and he didn't think, however much he changed, he ever would. Yet if it hadn't been for him and his absurd idea of revenging himself on her and Bob, they would never have married. She would probably have married some bright young man, and Bob would have married someone else and would probably—no, certainly—still be alive now. Everything was linked and interconnected and interdependent. And it was because of this fact, he decided finally, that he cared about Lenore, and that he suffered more and more the feeling that until her puzzle, as it were, was solved, her search successful, his own situation could never be resolved. He would never be released from Smith until Lenore knew—what?

Oh, but that was the problem.

A week after his first visit to her, he called her when he was out buying food and asked if he could see her again. She sounded surprised, but not very, as if she had imagined that he might call again but had thought it unlikely.

He arranged to meet her that evening at six, at her apartment. At five he dressed in his good suit—his other clothes needed to be pressed, he mentioned to Smith—and told the boy that he had forgotten to buy some milk that morning—which he had, on purpose—and was going out to fetch some.

Smith, watching the news on the television, gave him permission with a wave of his hand.

When he arrived at the menacing little apartment on Jane Street, Lenore gave him a glass of sherry—which he accepted and started drinking before he remembered that, with hepatitis, he shouldn't be touching alcohol—and asked if he minded listening to Prokofiev. It was the only thing that soothed her, she said. After a few minutes of the thin, spiky music, Fred thought he knew why.

But apart from this thought, which he kept to himself, he felt more sympathetic toward Lenore than he had ever felt before. He didn't like her any better, he just felt more sympathetic toward her. But that was a start, and was, in a way, so unexpected that he felt he was drinking sherry with someone he had never met before. It made him feel shy and awkward.

And Lenore too seemed strangely shy, or perhaps ill at ease. She apologized that she had nothing to offer him but sherry. She complimented him on his suit. She asked if he were feeling better, and told him that he certainly looked as if he was. She asked him when he was going back to work, and if he enjoyed his work. And finally, without a trace of suspicion, she asked him if he should be drinking. Fred told her, quite honestly, that he had forgotten he shouldn't.

"D'you want some more?"

"No," Fred said. "Better not."

They were, it occurred to him, like two shy young kids out on their first date together.

After they had sat in the apartment for three-quarters of an hour, Lenore asked Fred if he would have dinner with her. She was inviting him, mind you.

"Thank you," Fred said.

"You're welcome, O'Connor."

They went to a restaurant in Chinatown, and Fred let Lenore order for him. He said he didn't know what was good. In fact, as far as he remembered, he had never eaten a Chinese meal in his life.

"Well, it's about time you lived, O'Connor," Lenore said.

They talked the whole time—about the weather, about the mayor, about politics, about Lenore's family—and were both very quick to bring up a new subject the second a lull in the conversation or a meaningful silence threatened. They were both very conscious of the fact that they were talking about everything except the one thing they wanted to talk about, which was, of course, Bob.

But they didn't talk about him—they didn't even mention his name—until they had finished eating. Finishing their pale tea and enduring the menacing stare of the headwaiter, who wanted their table, they both knew the time had come.

Fred lowered his eyes and looked at the delicate little blue-veined teacup in his big red hands. "What are you going to do now, Lenore?"

"Work," the girl said. "I want to try and write another novel. I feel I'm ready for it now."

"Wouldn't it be better to wait awhile?"

"Probably. But without wanting to sound too—" she curled her upper lip expressively—"I want to see if I can get to the truth through fiction rather than fact, if you see what I mean."

Fred said he thought he did.

"Just the effort of forcing myself to be objective the whole time, to be absolutely ruthless about it, might get me to where I could never get by just thinking about myself and Bob and what I believe is the truth." The tiny plump fist clenched. "I must force everything into a pattern, and make it a *natural* pattern. Like a poet who is forced to find the precise word that rhymes can maybe express himself better that way—saying exactly what he wanted to say, or even more than he thought he wanted to say—than if he had used the word that first came into his mind. If you see what I mean," she repeated.

"There are people waiting for the table," the headwaiter said.

"So?" Lenore snapped.

When she had paid the check and they were walking outside, Fred said, "What you said about Bob last week— I've been thinking about it ever since. It's been worrying me." He looked down into Lenore's face and gave her a deep smile. "I wish I could tell you something. For my own peace of mind as much as yours," he added, truthfully.

"You wish you could but you won't, or you wish you could but you can't?"

"Because I can't," Fred said.

Fred walked Lenore home. When she asked him if he wanted to come up for coffee, he said yes; and when they were in the tiny apartment he turned the lights out and started to undress Lenore.

She said, "I don't know what the hell you're doing,

O'Connor," but she didn't stop him; and after they had made love, she lay with her elaborate hairdo on his chest, and cried.

And Fred too, as he lay on his back and stared up at the dark cracked ceiling, asked himself what the hell he was doing. It was a useless question. He knew quite well that he was trying, in some way, to destroy the past by reenacting it—to give both Lenore and himself a chance to take a different direction than the one they had taken. He was also trying, without actually saying the words, to tell Lenore what she wanted to know. He was trying to tell her that he had had a dream of the world very much as she had a dream of the book she wanted to write, and that Bob had learned about it, had stumbled into it, and had tried—at the cost of his life—to bring reality into it; to make it fact, rather than fiction.

It also occurred to him that perhaps it was just as well Bob was dead, because he was quite sure that even if he hadn't died, Lenore would have realized, quite soon, that their relationship was "meaningless," and would have written her book anyway. And as soon as she had done so, she would have discarded the empty chrysalis of the real Bob for the magic butterfly she had created.

He lay there, wanting to tell Lenore this, wanting to tell her to give up her dream as he had given up his; that otherwise slowly but surely, just as he had been dead in a way before, so she would die.

In their different ways, Lenore and he *were* alike; after all, they *had* had something fundamental in common. Which was why she had made love with him the first time, why she had rejected him so totally right after, and why she had made love with him again now. She understood him, and he made her, at least in part, understand herself. And so she rejected him.

At least, she *had* understood him. . . . But did she

158

understand him now? he wondered. Did she think he was still the same Fred as of old, or did she realize how far, how very far, he had come? No. Probably not.

She got up and started to dress; and as Fred too got up, she turned on the light and said, "You better get out of here, O'Connor."

It was what she had said four years ago; word for word. And her expression was the same expression she had worn four years ago. Fred wanted to stand up and shake her and say, "No, everything's different now." But he didn't. The past wasn't, couldn't be, so easily disposed of. Besides, he repeated to himself, as he dumbly dressed and left the apartment without a word, to have expected Lenore to understand everything would have been expecting too much. Far, far too much. . . .

He realized he was trembling as he opened the door of the apartment. What would Smith say to him? What would he do? Admonish him? *Punish* him?

He went into the living room and stood in front of the boy.

Smith looked him up and down and then laughed. "Well," he said, "did you have a nice evening with her?"

"How did you know?"

"Oh, Fred. I'm not a fool. As soon as I saw you getting dressed up I knew where you were going." Then, with his white monkey-hand, the boy waved him aside. "I can't see the television through you, you know."

Fred walked away, out of the room. He hung up the jacket of his suit, went into the kitchen, and made himself some coffee. Then he returned to the living room and sat down to wait for Smith to talk to him again. He was sure the boy hadn't finished.

He had to wait till the film was over. Smith got up at

last, turned off the television, sat down again, looked at him with a disdainful smile, and repeated, "Well?"

"Nothing," Fred said. "I didn't tell her anything. You needn't worry."

"Oh, *I'm* not worried," Smith laughed. Suddenly he looked at Fred anxiously, as if he had said what he shouldn't have and wondered whether Fred had noticed it.

He had. The boy had finally admitted it. He wasn't worried about being arrested for Bob's murder. He knew he could get out of it by telling the truth with the aid of a good lawyer, whom his grandmother would pay. He was staying here for reasons of his own; staying, as Fred had thought when Smith returned in tears the day after Bob's death, to see the end of the drama. Even to write the end of the drama himself.

And there was nothing Fred could do about it. Not any more.

"You realize," Smith drawled lazily on, "that when you do tell her, you'll have to kill her."

How easily he said it! As if he were telling Fred to go out and buy some milk. He *was* mad.

"And there's no need to look at me like that. I'm not mad. You will have to kill her, unless you want to go to prison for the rest of your life. Actually, I guess you'll have to kill her now anyway. You've gone too far."

Fred didn't say a word. It was as if he were listening to a murder mystery on the radio, he thought. He could get up and turn it off whenever he liked, only he didn't because he was, in spite of himself, fascinated and enthralled. The names of the characters in the radio play were names he recognized; they were his own name and Lenore's name!

Smith stood up and went over to the window. Looking out into the dark park, he said softly, "If you kill her, I'll go away. I'll go back to my grandmother's and risk whatever there is to be risked. I'll leave you in peace, Fred. And you'll have this place all to yourself again. It'll be just like it was before, only more so because there'll be nothing to disturb you. There'll be no danger, no risk at all. There'll be no one to threaten you, no one to menace you. You'll be all alone in your dream."

He turned now and faced Fred. "Are you trying to tell her, or at least trying to make her understand, just so you can—I mean—just so you *have* to kill her? Are you trying to find an excuse? A justification?"

Fred stared at the boy, hypnotized. He was mad, mad, mad. Talking about killing people. About killing plump, sour little Lenore. It was unthinkable. It was impossible. One couldn't kill people in real life. One could only kill people in dreams. As he had killed Bob. . . .

"I'm offering you your freedom," Smith said.

Fred went on staring at the boy for some time, and then, finally, he whispered, "Why?"

"Why what?"

"Why do you want me to kill her?"

"I don't *want* you to kill her. You have to."

"Why don't you just go away now and let me decide what I have to do?"

"Because if you tell this Lenore everything—" The boy shrugged. "Okay, I guess I could get off any murder rap or anything. I could say you were keeping me prisoner here all this time, and forced me to help you kill Bob—or to get rid of his body anyway—and that I ran away, but you chased after me and found me and brought me back here. But when I leave here I want to leave all this behind for-ever. I've been thinking a lot these last few days. I want to go back to school and get some good degree, and get a good job; one of my uncles is president of a bank in Los Angeles. You might have heard of him." Smith mentioned a name that Fred had heard of. "He could get me some

161

good job, I guess, and then I could settle down and get married and forget about all this—or at least put it down as a sort of boyhood adventure." He laughed now. "Because I figure you're right—no one *does* suspect me, so it's very unlikely there'd be any charges at all—so the only person in the world who would know would be you. And you'd be safely here in New York, keeping the peace and locked up in your dream palace. But if I leave you now, that cunt'll end up knowing everything. Apart from the scandal and the court case and everything, which wouldn't do my career or my reputation any good, though I guess I could survive, she'll make copy out of it. She'll write some goddamn book, or some of her articles, and I'll keep on cropping up in them, and she'll chatter to all her friends about me, and she'll always be after me, wanting details, wanting to know how I felt when I cut her precious husband's throat. I don't want any of that. I want the past to stop here, now, in New York. I want everything to come to a nice, tidy conclusion. My God, I'm not asking much. I'm offering you your freedom."

"Why don't you kill her yourself?"

"Because I've never killed anyone in my life, and I'm not about to start now. I wouldn't be able to go through with it."

"And if I just say no? If I let everything just ride—come to a natural end?"

Smith shrugged again, "I guess I would just stay here. But anyway, that's impossible. You know I'm right. You want to tell Lenore. Okay, fine. She already knows or suspects everything, I bet, even if she doesn't know what everything is. So you might as well tell her. Otherwise she'll pester and torment you until you do. But as soon as you have told her, you've got to kill her. I know that, and you know that, and maybe even she knows that. But if she wants to learn the truth that badly, that's her affair. You've *got* to kill her, Fred, or go to prison for life. You've got to. And you know it."

Fred put his hands over his face and muttered, "Will you turn out the light, please? It hurts my eyes."

Smith obliged.

And then Fred, in the dark, quiet room, lowered his hands and asked softly, "How do you think I should kill her?"

Two days later, according to plan, Fred called Lenore again. This time she didn't sound surprised at all, but merely as sour and as sharp as ever, with just a little extra something to let him know that she wasn't ashamed of having made love with him—by God, why should she be?—but that he'd better not try again, or even allude to the fact that they had.

"I can tell you what you wanted to know," he said when Lenore asked him why he wanted to see her.

That seemed to embarrass her. "What about?"

"About Bob."

"Oh." That seemed to embarrass her even more. "Well, can't you tell me now?"

"No," Fred said. "I—I'd like to tell you in person. Over the phone sounds sort of—" He stopped. How dramatic he sounded. How melodramatic. How absurd.

Lenore sighed. "Okay. When and where?" She no longer sounded embarrassed, just irritated now. Was this the way people always made appointments for their own deaths? Fred wondered, and he thought about what Smith had said: "Maybe even she knows." Was it possible?

He said, "Can I come around to your place this morning? In an hour or so?"

"Yes. Okay."

"I'll be around about twelve then."

"Okay," Lenore repeated. Then, as Fred was about to hang up, she said, "Hey, listen, O'Connor. Do me a favor."

"What?"

"Don't ask me to marry you."

At twelve o'clock precisely, Fred pressed the doorbell outside Lenore's house and was buzzed in without being asked who he was. And then, as he climbed the stairs and fingered Bob's gun, which was in his pocket, and loaded this time, he remembered Smith's instructions.

"Perhaps after all you shouldn't speak to her," the boy had said. "Don't tell her anything. Don't say a word. If you do, you're lost. I know you. Just wait till she's closed the door behind you, get out the gun, and shoot her in the right side of the head, holding the gun as close to her head as you can. And then—well, the rest's obvious. Put her hand around the gun and get the hell out. And try to make sure no one sees you. Though even if they do, I guess it doesn't matter. As long as they don't see you actually going in or coming out her door. You could always say you found the street door open, went up, rang her bell, and didn't find anyone at home. Anyway, no one's going to ask too many questions. Her husband gets killed, she can't stand it, she kills herself with her husband's gun. Okay?"

"Okay," Fred remembered that he had replied.

But it wasn't okay. It wasn't okay at all. Here he was on a damp, misty morning in April, while the rest of the world was shopping or working or sleeping, climbing the stairs to go and shoot a plump moustachioed girl in the head. What was more, he was supposed to shoot her without letting her say a word, without even explaining to her why she was dying. She was going to die in the penultimate chapter of her life, as it were, and would never know how the book ended. Maybe, Fred thought, that's the way we all die. But that didn't make it any better. It was horrible. It would be like stopping a piece of music just before it came to its climax, so that afterward all those unresolved notes and chords jangled about inside one, screaming, crying out for completion. It was horrible. It was madness. But he was going to do it. He had to. Smith had told him that he had to. . . .

How long it took to climb so few stairs! How long and long and long when those stairs were real stairs but one was pretending that they were only stairs in a dream. And how hard and steep they were. Oh, but he mustn't let himself think. He mustn't. He hadn't for the last two days, ever since Smith had told him what to do; and he mustn't now. This was all a dream, and soon it would be over.

But it was madness. . . .

"Are you okay, O'Connor?"

She was above him on the landing, in front of her open door, in her blue jeans and a gray sweater, her gray eyes looking defiantly at him. She had a pen in her hand.

What was he doing? he asked himself. What was happening? A boy called Smith had casually suggested that he go and kill a girl called Lenore, and he, just as casually, was going to do it. It wasn't possible. He felt himself swaying on the stairs, and heard only through a sort of veil Lenore's sharp voice saying, "For Chrissake, don't faint on the stairs. I couldn't hold you if I wanted to."

The voice only came to him veiled, but it was enough to stop him from fainting. He clung to it as if it were something palpable and managed to steady himself on it. Then he stood there—only three steps below Lenore—and smiled up at her.

"It's okay," he heard himself say. "I'm all right now." Then he climbed the last three stairs and put his hand on his forehead and murmured, "I guess I'm still sicker than I thought."

Lenore grabbed his arm, led him into the apartment, and closed the door behind him. He smiled at her again, but foolishly now, and thought that this was supposed to be it. But it wasn't, of course, because he still couldn't control himself. He could only let himself be led across the tiny room and pushed into the green armchair.

"Put your head between your legs," Lenore ordered. "I'll get you a glass of water."

She did, and he drank it, and then he lay back in the armchair and closed his eyes and breathed in deeply. He lay there, still, for what must have been about five minutes; slowly, as the oxygen returned to his brain, he began to feel better. He looked up at the cracked ceiling and thought that this apartment, like his own in Brooklyn, wouldn't be so bad after all with a bit of plaster and paint. Then he sat up straight in the armchair, smiled once more at Lenore as she gazed at him with an expression half of concern and half of irritation, and said, "I'm sorry."

Lenore nodded and muttered, "That's okay. It happens to the best of us."

"Yes," Fred said.

"You want another glass of water?"

"No. I'm fine now, thank you."

They looked at each other in silence for a while, Fred trying to decide what to do or say, and Lenore obviously torn between a desire to hear what he had to say and get him out of there, and a feeling that she'd better show some sympathy for a bit longer.

At last Fred said, "Lenore—"

"Yes?"

He closed his eyes again briefly and put his hand in his pocket. And then slowly, carefully, he took Bob's gun out. . . .

The gray eyes didn't even flicker. Good old Lenore, Fred thought. After all that had happened and in spite of

166

what Smith had said, in her neat edited world there was no room for violent death. Not her own, anyway.

He said, "Here, take it. It's Bob's. But be careful. It's loaded."

CHAPTER 10

But then, as she took it, there *was* fear in her eyes. There was fear, and doubt; and as she put it down on her work-table and spoke, there was fear and doubt in her voice too.

"How the hell did you get it?" she asked.

Slowly and very clearly, Fred said, "He left it in my apartment." And then, even as Lenore was saying, "What the hell was he doing in your apartment?" he added, more quietly, but even more distinctly, *"Our* apartment."

Then he lay back again in the chair and had the feeling of the most wonderful, profound relief. It was like being washed out to sea on warm waves, he thought; or perhaps, more, it was the feeling ice must have when it is released by the sun and can return to the streams, to the rivers, to the lakes; to flow out through the land once more and give life to crops and flowers and trees. Oh, it was wonderful, wonderful to be released. . . .

"Okay," Lenore said, sitting down on the Indian-cotton-covered divan, "explain."

"Do you think we can go out?" Fred murmured. "I need some air."

They went out and walked down damp Jane Street to the waterfront; and there, looking across to a New Jersey floating in the mist as delicately as an old Japanese village, Fred started to tell Lenore about his and Bob's relationship. He told her how he had spoken to Bob that day in the bar on Avenue B; of the sense he had had of finally being able to speak to someone who could understand him and possibly, in some way—he wasn't sure how—help him. He also told her how soon he had realized that this was not so, but that by then it had been too late.

"Too late for what?"

He told her about Bob's father dying of cancer—"I know that"—and needing money for an operation; he told her about Bob's corruption. He told her about Bob's suggestion that they buy an apartment, and he told her how they had bought it.

He didn't tell her where it was.

At this point, since the mist was clinging in droplets to their clothes and New Jersey was disappearing altogether, Lenore suggested that they go and have lunch somewhere together.

"But for God's sake let's go somewhere *normal*," she said. "I need familiar surroundings to hear this."

They took a taxi to Schrafft's on Fifth Avenue, and there, sitting in a booth—amid the dim grayness and shiny seats, the pale, heavy, unpainted Irish waitresses in their black dresses and white aprons, lumbering about—and over two vodka martinis ("Here's to hepatitis," Fred said weakly) he continued the story.

He told Lenore how, to get his own back, sort of, on Bob for having so taken him in that first day, he had insisted that they do nothing with their apartment, but just keep it as an empty monument to—

169

"To what?"

"I don't know. Just as—an empty monument."

Then he told Lenore how he had slowly fallen in love with the apartment; how it had come to obsess him; and how it had come to represent, in a way, his whole dream of the world.

He didn't tell her what his dream had been; strangely, he could hardly remember it.

He told her how they had both occasionally visited it; but that while Bob was always only a kind of guest, he himself ruled there, reigned there.

And then he told Lenore how he had felt when he met her, and how he had thought they had something profoundly in common. (Lenore didn't smile at this or even wince. She took it all in without a word.) And then he told her how, after Helen had left him, he had felt betrayed, and how he had planned his revenge on the two people he thought were responsible. He told her how he had introduced her to Bob with the intention of having her marry him—"Well, you know. You did." And, finally, he told her how, a couple of weeks before Bob died, he had bought out his share in the apartment.

And then he stopped talking and waited for Lenore to say something. But she ate a chicken salad before she spoke.

Then, with the air of getting her notes in order, she asked, "And the gun?"

"Just before he died, Bob called me in Brooklyn and told me he was going to the apartment to pick up the few things he had there. I went around this morning—it's the first time I've been since I got sick—and found the gun there. He must have left it. And then I just felt that I no longer loved that apartment, that I no longer wanted anything to do with it. And I thought it—the gun—was a sort of sign from Bob—to tell me that—I should tell you what you wanted to know." He bowed his big red head.

"Jesus, as they say," Lenore muttered.

"Please don't ask me where the apartment is," Fred said. "I can't—I mean I don't want to tell you." He tried a faint smile. "I guess I can't stop you from going to the police and telling them what I've told you about my corruption and the apartment, but obviously I'd prefer you not to. I mean—it wouldn't really do any good, would it? And there'd only be a lot of unpleasantness about Bob." He shrugged. "But I guess you must decide that."

"No," Lenore echoed him. "It wouldn't do any good. It wouldn't." She shrugged. "Do you want an ice cream?"

"No," Fred said. "But you have one."

Lenore raised a hand, and an Irish waitress approached. Oh, they had been right to come here, Fred thought. It *was* normal. Terribly, appallingly normal. A strange, old-fashioned normality, like a dream. A dream of Schrafft's . . . He suddenly started laughing.

Lenore raised her eyebrows, and he said, "I was just wondering if walls had ears."

"Oh, these walls must be deaf by now," Lenore muttered, looking at the gray businessmen and the pink-and-violet old ladies around them. "They must have died of boredom years ago. I'm sure a hundred murders are discussed here every day."

Fred stopped laughing and began, slowly, to stir his coffee. The word "murder" had brought him back to earth, had reminded him that his confession was incomplete. He shivered.

The word had obviously reminded Lenore of something, too. She said, "Just tell me—is this apartment anywhere near where Bob was killed?"

It was strange, Fred thought, that she hadn't been told that Bob was already dead when his throat was cut. But perhaps she had. Perhaps this was a trick. Perhaps she wasn't satisfied with his confession. Perhaps she realized he hadn't gone far enough. . . .

171

"No," he said. "Nowhere near."

Lenore ate her ice cream. When she had finished, she said, "If you bought out Bob's share, there should be a lot of money somewhere. What did you do? Give him a check?"

"Yes," Fred murmured. "But maybe he's got another checking account somewhere." He thought for a moment. "When you put the money down for your house in Connecticut—?"

"That was my money."

"Then," Fred said slowly, "I think Bob probably gave the money away. He said he would. He was very honest, you know."

Lenore lit a cigarette and sat back in the shiny plastic seat. She watched the smoke drifting up into the air. She watched it for a long time. And then, finally, she said, "Well, I guess it doesn't matter anyway."

"Are you satisfied?" Fred asked her gently.

"Satisfied?"

He flushed and, looking at the table, said, "I mean, have you had enough? To eat?"

"Oh, yes." Lenore watched the smoke again. And then she said, "But, no. I'm not satisfied."

Fred felt sweat on his hands. "How do you mean?"

"Well, you've told me all this, and it's all a sort of shock, obviously, even if at times—" She didn't finish her sentence. "Let's say you've filled in some gaps." She looked sharply at Fred. "But it's not enough. All this has got nothing to do with Bob's death. And there has to be some connection."

"Why? It was some maniac who killed Bob. Like all the others."

"No," Lenore said. "I don't believe that. I can't believe that. Even maniacs—and especially this one—have some method in their madness. There must be some connection. Some *pattern*."

"That's your literary mind at work," Fred said, with an attempt at a smile. "There's no connection. I just told you because I thought you wanted to know. And as for the apartment—well, Bob's death has made it kind of meaningless to me, and as you wanted to know—I know that there's a risk that you'll tell someone, but I thought that, as I was responsible in a way for you and Bob getting married—"

"You weren't responsible for that. We were."

"I know. But—"

"There *has* to be some connection between what you've told me and Bob's death. There is, anyway. He left his gun in this apartment of yours, and if he'd had it he might have been able to save himself."

"All the others who were killed were armed. It didn't save them."

"I know. But he might have been able to do something. And then the fact that he sold you his share in the apartment just before, as if he knew—"

"I tried for years to persuade him to sell me his share."

"Yes, okay, but the fact is that he *didn't* sell it until just before he was killed. And then you just said that now that Bob's dead the apartment has become meaningless to you; it's like what I said about our marriage. But why? You should be glad that Bob's dead. You hated him. You said so. The place should mean more to you than ever. No one in the world knew about it once Bob was dead."

"No. I was happy when Bob sold it to me. I didn't care if he knew. He would never have told anyone. He couldn't. But when he died—well, it was the fact that Bob had found the place, and gone into it with me. No. How could I be glad? His dying just made me see—" he shrugged—"the futility of the place, and of my hating him."

It sounded, he thought, very feeble.

Lenore must have thought so, too, because she said, "Let's get the check and get out of here." And then she added deeply, gravely, "I'm grateful for your having told me, Fred, but I wish you hadn't. Or if you had to, I wish you'd told me everything."

"So do I," Fred murmured. "But I can't. I don't know everything—if there is anything more to be known."

"Oh, there is," Lenore said. "There always is. I *know* there is. There has to be."

It was actually raining when they got outside; Fred stood silently on the edge of the sidewalk with Lenore, waiting for a taxi. As he looked down at the small, thoughtful girl, who had lit another cigarette and was biting one of her long nails, he realized that she was right. It would have been better to tell her nothing than to tell her only half the story.

A cab drew up, and as Lenore got in, he said, "I'm sorry, Lenore."

"Yep," she said, "and so am I. And now I must go home and think what to do about it."

So, Fred thought, must he. But then, as he waved to the girl—she didn't wave back; she wasn't even looking at him—he told himself that he knew what he would do about it. Smith had been right this time. Soon, quite soon, he *would* tell her everything. He would tell her everything even if he had to kill her afterward. But he didn't think he would kill her. After all, he had had his chance, and he had passed it up. No, he wouldn't kill her. He didn't want to kill her. He didn't want to kill anyone. He just wanted to tell her everything, and then be free.

Be free. What did it mean? How could he be free if he went to prison? But how could he be free if he didn't? Fred asked himself these questions, and others, as he walked slowly back to the apartment; but he could find no answers to them. All he managed to do, in fact, was confuse himself. By the time he got to his block, he was soaked to the skin, exhausted, and too totally worn out to think, let alone return the doorman's greetings.

Let fate take care of the future, he decided.

But when he got into the apartment there was an air about the place—a silence that, he immediately felt, required all his attention, all his faculties; and he forgot about his confusion, his weariness, his wet clothes, and fate, and all his nerves readied themselves to deal with whatever threatened. Like antennae, they reached out and sought to take in the invisible messages and meanings that hung heavily in the quiet dark air.

And these messages told Fred that Smith was no longer in the apartment. It was too quiet, too still, too altogether abandoned. The boy should have come out to meet him to see if he had accomplished his mission, or should at least have been watching the television. But the television was turned off, and there were no lights on anywhere, and there was—that silence.

He walked slowly down the corridor, holding himself stiffly, tensely, and no one jumped out at him. Smith had gone. He sat down in one of the armchairs and looked at the bare walls.

Smith had gone. . . .

Had the boy believed that he had killed Lenore, and left already? Was he already on his way back to his grandmother's big white house, to a few casual explanations and a future in banking? Had he been scared that something would go wrong and decided that he'd better get out while he had the chance? Fred didn't know. And as he sat, motionless, in the empty room, and looked through the windows at the sky that now was showing traces of blue, it suddenly, and briefly, occurred to him that maybe Smith had never existed at all. Maybe the boy had been a dream, the embodiment, as Bob had suggested, of his conscience, come to haunt him, taunt him, and lead him to what he was now: a big red man, sitting all alone. . . . But, no. That was ridiculous. Smith had existed, all right. Bob's death was the proof of it. Bob's death and his own present condition—which was not, he told himself, that of a man sitting all alone, but that of a man waiting on the edge of freedom, just gathering his strength and breath for that final crossing of the frontier. Yes, Smith had existed, all right—but now he existed no longer. Just as, very soon, this apartment would exist no longer. Both of them, the boy and the eight or nine empty rooms, would belong only to the past; to a captive, dead past that he would have cast off forever. Oh, how he longed for that time! When everything could be thrown away; when everything, everything in the world, would be new. What a wonder it would be to see a blade of grass for the first time, or a tree, or, even more perhaps, a living human being: a weak, guilty human being struggling to live, to accept compromise and disappointment, to love, to do all the things that a human being could and had to do while he or she was so briefly alive. Oh, what a wonder it would be. . . .

Meanwhile, he sat quite still in the room and gazed at the walls and the ceiling and the greenish-brown carpet, and whispered goodbye to them, and told them silently that he hoped whoever lived among them next would be happy.

He sat there for an hour, maybe more, and outside the sky was becoming bluer and bluer and the clouds whiter and whiter as they were lit by the afternoon sun. He would wait for the sun to set, he thought, and then he would call Lenore for the last time. He sat there with a gentle smile on his face and wished, just for a second, that he had a mirror with him. He would have liked to look in it. He was sure that what he would have seen would have been beautiful. Yes. He, big, ugly, red O'Connor, would have been beautiful. . . .

But he didn't have a mirror, and so he simply sat there looking at the blue sky, waiting for the sun to set.

He was still sitting, looking out the window, when suddenly he heard a noise—a noise that made him sit up, rigid with shock and fear, and made the hairs on the back of his red neck stand on end. It was a strange, gurgling, strangled noise; but it was a noise that was coming from somewhere near. From somewhere very near. And there was no mistaking what it meant.

There was someone in the apartment. . . .

It was impossible, he told himself wildly. There couldn't be. Not now. Not when everything was over, finished. Not when peace had finally, after a lifetime of waiting, come to him. There couldn't be!

And then, as the panic spread through him, he wanted to shout out loud. No! There mustn't be. Let him be mistaken. Let there be no noise. Please, please, he wanted to shout, let there be no noise. Let me be having a dream now, the most terrible nightmare that anyone has ever had. But let there be no noise.

But there was; and as he sat quivering, sweating, cold in his chair, he heard it again. And it *was* the noise—though it was weird, muffled, obscene—of a human being. He knew he had to do something about it. He had to go out and meet it.

Quietly, breathlessly, he got to his feet and tiptoed to the door of the living room.

The noise was coming from down the corridor.

Quietly, breathlessly, he moved toward it.

It was coming from the slightly open door of the bath-room.

Quietly, breathlessly, he moved toward it and pushed the door open.

And then, as he saw what was in there, though he didn't make a sound, he heard a scream within him that was like the scream of a soul being forced through the furthest limits of agony. It was like the scream of a man who had finally come face to face with the Furies. He couldn't bear it. It was going to deafen him. His head was going to explode. He closed his eyes, and bit his lips, and pressed his hands to his ears. But it was all no use. The scream went on and on, getting louder and louder, becoming more and more unbearable. And then it started to fade.

And as it faded Fred lowered his hands and opened his eyes and looked once more into the bathroom. There, lying on the floor, he saw Smith. A completely naked Smith, with white flaky skin and watery blue eyes, red around the rims. A Smith whose feet were tied with a piece of cord, whose hands were locked in front of him with a pair of handcuffs, and whose completely shaven head was bound up with surgical tape.

Fred sat down on the floor of the corridor and stared. He was too shocked, too stunned to move. He simply sat there and stared. He knew he should get up and release the boy, but he couldn't. He should take the tape off the boy's head and ask him what had happened; what grotesque, appalling trick of time or reality had been played on them. But he couldn't move. What did it mean? What could it mean? He sat there, and stared, and asked himself these questions again and again, until, eventually, he felt capable of standing up. He stood up and took a step toward the boy, still asking himself what it could mean, and still incapable of thinking.

But just as he was about to remove the tape from the boy's head, the doorbell rang. His doorbell. It rang in exactly the same way as it had the day Smith had first come. And as it rang, jangling through the apartment and through him, he suddenly knew what had happened. Not all the details, not all the exact moves, but he knew the overall idea. He knew what had happened, just as he knew who was at the door—and just as he knew that there was nothing in the world he could do about it. Nothing, except go to the door and open it.

He left Smith lying on the floor and walked down to the hallway. He didn't hesitate for a second. And when he had opened the door and seen little plump Lenore, with her gray eyes and her moustache, standing there with Bob's snub-nose .38 pistol in her hands (how nervously but how strangely well she held it; much better than her husband had), all he said was "Hi."

"Where is he?" Lenore said bluntly.

Fred wanted to smile at her and tell her she could put the gun away. It wasn't necessary. But he knew she wouldn't believe him, and anyway what did it matter? Let the comedy end as it would.

"He's in the bathroom," he murmured, and turned and put his hands in the air and led the way down the corridor.

When she saw Smith, Lenore said, "Jesus!"

Fred thought the exclamation was what someone might have said in a film or in a book. But that wasn't surprising under the circumstances. Lenore was playing a part in a book.

He really thought he should congratulate her on her confidence and style; after all, she couldn't ever have done anything like this before. Still pointing the gun at him, she tore the surgical tape off Smith's head with her free hand, managing to do it more brutally than he ever had. And then she untied his feet.

179

"Where's the key to the handcuffs?" she asked Fred.

Fred was about to say that he didn't know, but Smith drawled flatly, "He always keeps it in the closet down the corridor there, on the first shelf."

Lenore went down the corridor backwards, so she could keep Fred covered, opened the closet door, found the keys, came back, and released Smith's hands. He rubbed his wrists and got up.

"Can you keep that on him," he said to Lenore, pointing at the gun, "while I get some clothes on?"

Lenore nodded. And then Fred saw she was trembling, and he realized that she was, in spite of her apparent confidence, terrified. It wasn't surprising, he guessed. Poor thing. This wasn't really her sort of scene at all. It was much too messy. Still, later, and with a bit of careful editing, she would be able to make it—well, readable, if not quite believable.

She stood and faced Fred for five minutes—he kept his eyes lowered, not wanting to embarrass her—until Smith returned, wearing his blue blazer and a white shirt and black pants and a tie, and looking for all the world—apart from his shiny, shaven head—like a nice, rich young college graduate, going for an interview for a job he was sure he would get. Which, reflected Fred, quite soon he would be.

"Okay, I'll take it if you like."

Lenore passed him the gun—he held it even better than she had; lazily, easily, like one born to hunting—and fished in the pocket of her baggy white wool cardigan for a cigarette, which she lit with an audible sigh.

"Shall I go call the police now?" she said.

"You'll have to go down to the superintendent's office. He cut the wires of the phone here."

"I'll go upstairs," Lenore said, "and call from there. That's where I'm supposed to be anyway." She managed a sour smile at Smith. "My friends didn't know what was going on. I got the doorman to call them. I went up, told them I had to see someone else and would be back soon, and came down here. They thought I'd gone mad. But I couldn't think of any other way of getting into the building without having the doorman call up here. And you said I shouldn't."

And now Smith smiled at her, but patronizingly, patricianly. "Wouldn't you like to hear the whole story before the police come? Because once they get on to it you're only going to hear bits and pieces."

Lenore seemed doubtful—she looked from Smith to Fred and back again—and then, the artist in her winning over the dutiful citizen, she said, "Okay. You don't think he's—?" She shrugged.

"Oh, he's all right now. He knows it's all over. But let's go into the living room and sit down."

Lenore looked even more doubtful, but Smith was so very much in charge, so very much the gracious host in his town apartment, that she nodded and repeated, "Okay."

Fred led the way to the living room, and stood there, still, while Lenore and Smith sat down. He saw the girl's gray eyes flickering around, taking notes. They would come in useful, he guessed.

Smith, once again, gave a soft little smile. "Well, I guess I should explain a few things first. I mean—I didn't tell you anything on the phone, did I?"

"No," Lenore said.

"Well—" He giggled. "I guess I'm sort of crazy. But I've always had this thing about guilt. You know—crime and punishment and that sort of thing. I've always wanted to know exactly what a guilty person felt like. You know. Really get into their minds, and feel like they feel. I mean—how would you feel if you'd killed someone? I guess I wanted to know because I thought that if I really

181

could understand—well, I'd understand a whole lot about human nature, and myself."

Fred glanced at Lenore and saw that it was her turn now to look patronizing and slightly scornful. He remembered Smith's grandmother saying, "Leo's silly."

"Anyway, it was only a sort of fascination—a hobby, if you like—though once, up in Providence, I did go and confess to the police that I'd raped and killed some girl who was found there. I did it just to see the mechanics of an arrest and an interrogation and all that sort of thing. And also to see if just by being arrested I could make myself guilty." He giggled again. "I couldn't, unfortunately. They never believed me for a minute. They called my grandmother—I live with my grandmother—and she came and took me home. Anyway," the boy repeated, "last year—well, the end of the year before last, I guess it was, after the second of the cop killings—I started to get fascinated with the idea that here was some guy going around killing cops. And I tried to get into the mind of the murderer. I thought, If I was the Cop Killer, what would I do? How would I go about it? What would I be like? And I really thought about it, and studied it. And I was sure that the Cop Killer—like some of the papers said—was a cop himself. Someone who had something to hide. Because I know—I mean I guess everyone knows—that all the cops in the Narcotics Bureau are wide open to bribes and corruption and—everything. So I really put myself into the shoes of this unknown murderer and tried to think as I thought he would think. I tried to find a pattern, tried to imagine everything. I came down to live in New York, and took an apartment in the East Village, and—started to try to live the life of the murderer, let's say. I went out at night and wandered the streets; I followed as many different cops in the Narcotics Bureau as I could, to pick the next victim, and—" He sighed. "Right before the third murder I found

Fred here. And as soon as I saw him—I knew. I was convinced. And I couldn't think why everyone else didn't know, too. It was obvious. Just by looking at him. And then he was always alone when he wasn't working, and—like I say, it was obvious. And I started to follow him, and find out about him—who he was, how he lived, where he lived. And quite soon I discovered—this place. And this was the secret I knew he must be protecting. Killing for. And then—I just watched. I didn't see him actually kill any of the cops, but once I was only two minutes behind him. I guess I should have gone to the police, but I thought that if they didn't know maybe there was no proof, and—anyway, I didn't. But then I thought that I'd like to meet him. Just so I could really see at first hand what a guilty person was like. I came here a couple of times and he wouldn't let me up, and then I tried to speak to him outside, in the subway once. And then finally I came here and—I guess I knew I was running a big risk—I mean I *did* know. But I thought that it was worth it. Because I thought that if I came here, not only would I be able to see the real—heart of darkness, but also, eventually—if he didn't kill me, and I took as many precautions against that as possible—he would end up giving himself away. He would end up confessing. And so that way I was doing something good. Because if I—or someone—didn't force him to confess, he might go on killing forever." He sighed again. "He kept me prisoner here—like you saw. He treated me like a dog. But he couldn't kill me, because I'd left his name and address and all the details about him in a notebook at my grandmother's house. He went up and got that notebook—and that was one of the few times I was really scared—but then I realized he'd spoken to my grandmother, and if I was found dead she'd give a description of him and he'd be caught. No. I was fairly safe. But I'd made one mistake. I'd always assumed he'd taken this place by himself." He

183

lowered his eyes. "I didn't know about your husband. But one day he came here and discovered me and—he killed him. He knocked him out here, and then took his body to the natural history museum and cut his throat. He made me help stretch the body out. And then—he tried to shoot me, but the gun wasn't loaded, and I ran away. That's when I bumped into that guy. I ran into Central Park. But he followed me and found me and brought me back. But I managed to persuade him that you suspected him. That's why he's been coming around to see you. And today he said he was going to kill you. My God, I was desperate. But there was nothing I could do except wait. And then he came back and said he had lost his nerve. That he hadn't been able to do it—and that everything was over for him. He unlocked my hands and took the tape off my face. And then he went to another bathroom and took a shower. And while he was taking it I crept down the corridor and looked up your name in the book—and told you to come here. That was why I was whispering. I didn't call the police—and I didn't want you to come with the police—because I thought that if they came battering on the door, or he heard sirens, he might panic and kill me. Just as a last act, kind of. I thought if you came alone and rang the door-bell—well, he'd either think it was one of the doormen, come up for some reason, or—if he asked who it was, and you said—he'd let you in. Because, as he'd lost his nerve before when he tried to kill you—" Smith shrugged. "I guess Freud would say he let me go for those five minutes because he wanted me to call someone—he knew that since he'd lost his nerve with you it was all up. Because as soon as he had finished taking his shower he came back and tied me up again—and maybe suspected about the phone, because he suddenly went and cut the wires. But it was all like shutting the stable door after the horse had bolted—and he had wanted it to bolt. I couldn't get out the door

184

because he always keeps it locked with a key, and he had the key with him. But anyway—here you are, and this is the end of the story, and here's the man who killed your husband, and here's—the Cop Killer."

Fred had been watching Lenore throughout Smith's long explanation—watching her disinterestedly, objectively, as if he had nothing to do with what was being said—and he could see that she wasn't entirely happy with the boy's story. But he could also see that, while she might not be satisfied with all the particulars, she believed the basics of it; and he guessed that she would probably believe the whole of it when she had thought it over and done a bit of careful editing and rewriting. Just as the police, when they came, would believe it. . . .

And why not? he thought. It could have been true. And anyway, what did it matter? He couldn't fight Smith, and Lenore, and the rest of the world, nor did he even want to any more. He had wanted freedom, and here was freedom, of a sort, being offered him. And he wasn't in a position to beg or choose.

He was suddenly immensely, terribly tired. He just wanted to get everything over and put an end to it. He wanted to let Smith out of here, let him go and do his explaining and have his brief moment of lurid publicity—although perhaps his grandmother would be able to keep his name out of the papers—and go and pursue his banking career; and he wanted to let Lenore go and return to her tiny apartment and her neat little articles and books. Let them return to their dreams and try to find comfort in them, and forget all that had happened in the past. Let them go out into their cold, ordered world, if that was the world they wanted. But just let them go, and leave him to *his* world, and to the freedom he had at last found.

"Is it true?" Lenore murmured, with just a trace of doubt in her voice. "Is that all true, Fred?"

Fred looked out the window at the afternoon sky that was now completely and beautifully blue. What did it matter? he asked himself again. Let them have their truth, if that was what they wanted. He had his own, and he was too tired to try to impose it on them.

"Yes," he said slowly. "It's all true. I killed them all." And then, as if in a trance, he recited all the details of the killings. Exactly as he had read them, and now quite distinctly remembered them, in Smith's notebook. "It's all absolutely true. About Bob, and all the others. And I'm glad it's over."

And then, almost sleepwalking, he went across the room and opened one of the windows. He heard Lenore make a sort of gasp behind him, so he turned, said softly, "It's all right, I'm not going to throw myself out," and smiled at the girl, as if to reassure her and remove any last trace of doubt that might remain within her, doubt which, if it weren't removed, would torment her always and possibly one day destroy her. And he didn't want that. . . . Then he turned back to the window and looked down at the green lovely park—the perfectly planned and lovely park in which it was unsafe to walk at night—and said weakly, "I'm just letting in the spring."

As soon as Lenore had gone upstairs to her friends' to call the police, Fred, more from a sense of decency and tidiness than real curiosity, said to Smith—who lowered his gun now, and was smiling at him—"So it was you after all?"

"I *told* you so," the boy said, coyly and enigmatically. And then, with the air of one who is telling a fairy tale—which, Fred reflected, it was still just possible that he was—Smith went blandly on. "I killed the first two because I wanted to really know what it felt like to be guilty. I chose them both from the Narcotics Bureau because it was

186

sort of easier, and neater, and I'd been reading a book about some cops in the Narcotics Bureau. And then, just when I was trying to pick my third victim, I came across you. And—like I told Lenore here, and like I said in my notebook—as soon as I saw you I *knew* that you were the right person. I knew that one day, when I had finished—" he giggled—"doing my research into human nature, I was going to get sick of it, and would want to settle down and lead a normal, decent life. And I knew that you were the person who would, if I was careful, and clever, confess. You see," he said, "I *know* about guilt and the guilty. You would have confessed anyway, sooner or later, to whatever I had done, but your killing Bob just speeded everything up. Except, of course, that you didn't kill Bob. I did. He wasn't dead when I cut his throat, and I haven't even got the excuse that you were pointing a gun at me, because I knew it wasn't loaded. Your precious friend Bob, when we were waiting for you, told me he never kept his gun loaded, under any circumstances. He said he'd never killed anyone, and never could, and would rather die himself than do so. He did." Smith laughed.

"I'm still guilty of killing him," Fred muttered.

"Oh, for Chrissake. You sound like me," Smith said. "No, you're not. You knew that Bob never loaded his gun, too—he told me you knew—and you could never have cut his throat yourself."

Fred shrugged. It was a technical point, he guessed; an academic question for people—other people—to argue over.

"I was never scared of your killing me," Smith continued. "In fact I wanted you to try—that first day I was here. Because I knew you'd have lost your nerve, and as soon as you had—well, you were mine. But I kept the notebook as a sort of guarantee. Maybe the only time I was really scared was when I ran away after killing Bob and bumped into that guy. Then I really thought I'd had it—or we'd both had it. I was sure that they would find us. But they didn't," he said lightly. "And I guess I was sort of scared after you didn't even try to kill me, and when you kept me tied up here, because I thought, My God, it's going to take a year to wear him down, to get under his skin and disturb him until he cracks. I thought I'd bitten off more than I could chew. I mean—I really couldn't stand it, being kept like a dog. But, as I say, Bob's death speeded everything up. And then today—I knew you'd never kill Lenore either. I knew you'd tell her something, though, and I guessed just how much. Just in case you told her everything and she told the police, I took the precaution of shaving my head and tying myself up so I'd be found like that when they came. I mean, I would have done that anyway, because Lenore had to see me like that, but—I didn't want you to tell her everything, because I was scared that even if you told her about Bob you might not have told her about all the others. Though I guess if she'd asked, you would have. You were just dying to confess, weren't you?" Then the boy stood up and pointed the gun at Fred again. "I really do know about guilt now, don't I?" He smiled, and then added mockingly, "And I'll tell you what I've discovered, Fred-o. That guilt is a dreadful thing. It's guilt that ruins the world—that's destroying this country and everything that's good in it."

How bitter the words sounded, like a north wind blowing in from the past.

"But there are always enough weak people around to offer themselves up as sacrifices so the rest of us can keep going. The innocent weak. God bless you, Fred."

"I'm not innocent," Fred said earnestly. "Even if—about Bob—but I mean—for years I've been more or less helping sell drugs that were destroying people. And—"

"Oh, being innocent doesn't mean not doing anything wrong, I don't think," Smith said glibly. "And anyway, even if you haven't been an angel in the past—you'll do now. In fact, you'll do perfectly, Fred. Just perfectly." And with that, and a laugh, the boy turned and walked quickly out of the room.

Fred didn't move—where was he to move to? he thought—but simply stood there, waiting for Smith to return, which he would do almost immediately, he guessed. He couldn't, he wouldn't, leave him alone. . . .

He didn't. But when he returned, practically running, Fred saw that he was carrying the bread knife he had bought after Bob's death, and which had never been used. . . .

"We better get on with it," Smith said, nervous now at last. "Otherwise Lenore will be back." Then he handed Fred the bread knife and went on, "Remember, though, when they ask you in heaven how it happened, you say that you asked me if you could have a glass of water, and I said yes. But when you got into the kitchen you grabbed the bread knife and—bop." The boy made a gesture with his white hand.

For a second, as he realized what was expected of him, Fred felt he should protest—or should even refuse and force Smith to shoot him if necessary. But then he thought, Why? Why waste breath? Why spoil everything at this stage? Why not just go along with it? And besides—what other way was there? And hadn't he, for some time now, known it must end like this? Oh, yes. And he was even strangely glad. Because he was so very tired, and had come such a long, long way. Still, he had one last request.

Wearily, softly, he asked, "Can we do it here? So I can look out the window?"

Smith considered for a moment. "I guess so," he said eventually. "I can always say you grabbed the bread knife and ran back in here and I didn't dare shoot you."

"Thank you," Fred murmured, getting down on his knees and taking the bread knife in his right hand.

"You're welcome," Smith laughed. "After all, it's the

least I can do for you. Because, like I said—you're not a bad guy, Fred. I mean really, you're one of the best."

"Thank you," Fred murmured again. He looked down at the bright shining knife in his big red hand, up at the blue spring sky that was now pouring in through the open window, and then back at Smith. "Will you help me please?" he whispered.

Smith frowned. "Oh, no," he said. "I can't. *I've* never killed anyone. I mean—you're the Cop Killer, aren't you?"

"Oh, yes," Fred whispered. And then, taking a last look up at the window, and the blue sky that now was pouring into him—pouring into his eyes, his blood, his brain—pouring into him, soothing him, thawing any last vestige of ice that might remain anywhere within him—he lifted the knife and pulled it, very hard, across his throat.